LAST BREATH

LINCOLN CHASE

LAST BREATH

First Edition: January, 2020
ISBN: 978-0-9768974-9-1

Design Vault Press, LLC

www.designvaultpress.com

For my lake tribe. You know who you are.

PROLOGUE

July 15, 1993 … 4:35 a.m.

The grass was thick with dew, soaking through the elastic cuffs of her pajama pants. She was on the edge of sleep, less than half awake. Too drowsy to register the miles she'd traveled, the faraway bruising of her tender feet. A boy shuffled by in the darkness, grazing her shoulder in passing. There were others too, but Carrie scarcely noticed; the voice overwhelmed all but the edge of her senses.

The water, it sang in her ear.

Yes… the water. The water would be warm.

Come to me, child. Come to the water. You must hurry.

Gradually, the sound of water lapping against the shore crowded in, beckoning her in a soothing cadence. The lake glistened mere feet ahead, now. A riot of birds flocked above, the thunder of their wings compelling her onward. She let her eyes slide closed and trundled blindly ahead. Her feet plunged ankle-deep into the lake; it felt good.

With a sleepy smile, the girl surged beyond the shallows. All around her, the water churned with movement. Arms and legs broke the surface, some brushing against her, others carrying her out by their momentum. Abruptly, the lake floor dropped away. She sank into the depths in a sigh of bubbles.

And then, Carrie slept.

CHAPTER 1

July 8, 2018 ... 4:04 p.m.

Just passin' through?"

I wasn't, but I'd just as soon keep that to myself. Not that I was a fugitive or anything, to clarify; but that's not to say I wasn't on the run. From what or where to was still up in the air.

The florist pursed her lips and rang up my arrangement without another word. An overpowering mismatch of floral perfume—the same I might've associated with romance in a different time and place—all but overpowered me in the confined space, smothering me like a sickly-sweet pillow. I couldn't get my wallet out fast enough.

The woman's relentless gaze burned holes through me as I laid three twenties on the counter and scooped up the flowers. "Thanks," I muttered and headed for the door.

She recognized me, of course, even if she was a stranger to me.

Hard to forget a face like mine—long and pale, punctuated by an unruly shock of black hair. Everyone in this little town knew who I was, even if they played dumb for the sake of propriety—a kindness the locals bothered with less and less, incidentally.

I dredged up the past every time I showed my face in Langley, Oklahoma. Twenty-five years of grief, dead and buried by all rights, resurfaced on their faces when I walked by; experienced anew as if not a single day had passed. They hated me.

Hell, I didn't blame them. *I* hated me.

Just as I reached the exit, all but gasping for fresh air, the woman spoke again. "You keep comin' back here," she said. Not an inquiry as to why, or even a polite observation. There was a jagged edge on her tone, like an accusation. Like I came back just to hurt people. I'd learned long ago to embrace the sting and let it pass; allowing it to fester gave it undeserved power.

I stole a glance at her over my shoulder. The usual knee-jerk apology was on my lips, but I bit it off. I was tired of shouldering the emotional wellbeing of a town that despised me. "I do," I agreed. "I keep coming back."

She glared at me, her mouth twitching.

"You'd prefer that I didn't."

The woman swallowed. "Yes."

Quivering in the recesses of my gray matter, a gear abruptly clinked into position; my gaze dropped to the flower arrangement, from which a card protruded on a plastic trident.

Lola's Petals & Stems.

The name hadn't registered until now. "Lola," I muttered. "Lola Simpson?"

A shadow flurried across the woman's face, but she didn't reply. She didn't need to. I took a closer look around. The storefront was dated, but what could be tastefully decorated had been. *Small-town chic*, a hip out-of-towner might've dubbed it. Fitting homage to the girl long lost; she would've liked it.

"I was born here, same as Lola," I pointed out. "Even if I don't live here anymore, it'll always be home."

The woman's lips thinned, but she held her tongue. When her eyes turned to glass and flicked away, I felt my empathy yawn, stretching cramped little limbs. It didn't get much action in St. Louis. It wasn't needed. "Lola was a nice girl. I hate to cause anyone pain," I said, and left before she could reply.

It was as close to an apology as I could muster that day for being who I was. Not a criminal, not a person of unsavory ethics. Not someone who had ever done anything particularly regrettable, in fact, much less something that warranted the forgiveness of a stranger. My only crime?

I was the lucky one. The sole survivor.

Coming back here was hardly my idea of fun, by the way. Truth is, returning to my hometown hurt me as much as it hurt the townsfolk. My mom was in the home stretch, you see, with mere days left. She was the only thing still tethering me to this town.

Almost, anyway.

Basking in the fresh air with my windows down, I drove through town a few miles under the speed limit, noting with sadness that the eclectic retail stores and hole-in-the-wall restaurants I'd known and loved as a kid had thinned to a sparse few; even those bore the unmistakable hallmark of floundering commerce.

I pulled up to the house with nerves burning at the back of my throat, instinctively dodging potholes that seemed to reappear every year, no matter how many times they were filled in. I parked behind my mother's Buick Regal, which was hemmed in by a fringe of un-trimmed grass. It probably hadn't been driven in months.

The front door glided open on groaning hinges. "Hello?"

No answer, which wasn't surprising. Also not surprising, my mom was in bed. Seeing her there, lying still with such resignation, put a hitch in my breath. An oxygen cannister was propped against the wall where the headboard met sheetrock, its facemask and air hose draped lazily over the pressure nozzle. That it wasn't in use said a lot; my mom was no longer fighting. She'd given up.

I hadn't returned with any hope for a miracle, in case you're wondering; I came home to send her off. I loved my mother dearly, but it was time. She'd suffered long enough.

With a stomach in knots, I put the flowers in a vase and placed them on her nightstand, nudging a worn paperback aside to make room. Her bedroom—once cluttered by the colorful treasures of a woman whose curiosity knew no bounds—was now a forlorn space. Devoid of color, any attempt at décor—however unconventional—had been overtaken by pharmacy bags and piles of religious maga-zines. Pill bottles and tissue boxes.

Taking one of her frail hands in mine, I bent at the waist to kiss it. Her mottled skin was frightfully thin, the inner structure of her hand peeking through as if wrapped in wet tissue paper.

I wished my dad was still around. He'd know what to do, what to say. You can learn things in the classroom or from books. You can devote a lifetime to scholarly pursuits. But none of that amounts to a damn at times like this. PhDs and certifications—they lose all value at death's door. For all his faults, my dad got that more than most. More than me, anyway.

I felt the weight of my mom's gaze on me, but I couldn't bring myself to return it yet. I was on the verge of tears and didn't want her to see me like that. One of us had to be strong, and for once, I wanted it to be me.

"I knew you'd come," she whispered.

I opened my mouth to reply, but nothing came out.

"Look at me, Shane," she whispered. "Let me see those baby blues."

I hesitated but obliged just as a tear broke ranks to streak down my cheek. I caught it on the back of my hand and forced a smile.

Her brow furrowed. "What happened to your eye?"

"Nothing, Mom. It's fine."

"You've been fighting."

"Don't worry about it. I'm fine."

Her eyelids slid shut and she fell silent. For a while, I thought she'd fallen asleep. But then she swallowed audibly, and her eyes shot open again. "Shane," she wheezed. "It isn't over—you know that, don't you?"

I wish I could say she was voicing a general observation about life after death, but I knew better. "It'll be fine, Mom."

"It's gonna happen again. Soon."

I nodded, even if I wasn't entirely convinced.

"I want you to leave this place, son. When I'm gone, call a realtor and sell the house. Use the money for whatever you want, but... don't come back here again."

I squeezed my eyes shut. "I can't promise that, Mom."

"Of course you can."

She didn't understand. How could she? She and my dad had split when I was sixteen, an event that unleashed a transient streak in my dad. Almost overnight, he became restless, a late-blooming nomad who simply couldn't bear to linger in one place for long. When the hatred of this town became unbearable, I left here—the place of my birth—to follow him all over Arkansas and Missouri. I told myself it would be an adventure, but it wasn't. It was a sickness, constantly running from something that couldn't be outrun.

True, I had an apartment and a job now. Yet as much as I was hated here, this place was still the closest I had to a real home. My roots were torn and stunted, yet here they remained.

I gave her hand a gentle squeeze and rose to my full height. "I'm gonna check in with Winnie."

My mom coughed weakly and tried to smile. "Oh, good. She'll be thrilled to see you."

I crossed the empty stretch of yard between the house and my aunt's bedraggled RV, a path worn smooth by daily use over the years. Despite my mother's prediction, Winnifred was not at all thrilled to see me. On the contrary, her cheeks darkened to deep crimson when she saw me at her door.

"Goddammit, Shane," she snapped, lunging to her feet and sending the entire RV into a seismic wobble. "I asked you not to come."

"In your letter," I growled through the screen.

Storming to the door and yanking it open, Winnie towered over me. "Yes, in my damn letter."

"You didn't think Mom's condition was worth a phone call? What if she'd passed away while your letter was in the mail?"

Winnie glowered and planted meaty hands on her hips. She was wearing a t-shirt emblazoned with the phrase MY EYES ARE UP HERE, and under any other circumstances, I'd have cracked a smile. "What if?" she spat. "You'd swoop in to sell the house and send me packin'."

My lips parted in surprise. "Is that what this is all about? The *house*? Oh, my God, Winnie. I don't even want it."

She blew a raspberry. "Uh-huh. I don't believe that for a second."

My cheeks seemed to catch fire. "Why would you even think that? What have I ever done to make you think about me like that?" I couldn't help the wounded note in my voice.

My aunt's eyes veered off to nowhere. "You've been gone a long time, Shane. People change."

I appraised her for a long moment before producing a thick envelope from my back pocket. In my irritation, I was tempted to rip it to shreds and piss all over it. But I kept my cool, handing the envelope off to Winnie and leaning against the RV's retractable step railing. She tore into it and unfolded a sheaf of pages—ten, to be precise—and began to read, her eyes flicking up to mine every few paragraphs. Her cheeks paled.

"This for real?"

"Yeah, Winnie."

Her lips puckered and her chin dipped dubiously toward her chest. "Been taking your medicine?"

That hit me like a knee to the nuthatch. Few things pushed my buttons harder than someone questioning my ability to make rational decisions just because I used to take pills. Truth is they hadn't done a damn thing for me anyway, other than numb my senses.

I did my best to tamp down a geyser of fury. "Don't do that, Winnie. I've been off meds for a long time. You know that."

Winnie blinked and let the papers fall to her side. Emotion porpoised in and out of her features, betraying just how trying these last few months must've been on her. "Shit," she sighed. "I'm sorry, Shane. I forgot."

This did little to mollify me, but I managed a curt nod.

"But your mom… she left the house to *you*, Shane." Tears sprang to her eyes and she tried to blink them away. "I–I've seen the will."

"I know, I've seen it, too. Hence the document in your hand. It's a bill of sale. She wants me to sell the house, anyway."

Winnie's eyebrows narrowed. "And you want to sell it to me."

I nodded coolly, cringing inwardly under the sting of her suspicious nature, which—until that day—had never been leveled on me.

"But… for a dollar? You can't do that, Shane."

"Sure I can. I'd prefer to just give it to you, but apparently it's easier this way."

Her mouth snapped shut like a steel trap.

I gave the RV a stiff rap with my knuckles. "You've settled for this thing long enough, don't you think?"

I'd never understood what fueled her to stay in that cramped space when there was plenty of room in the house. I'm sure there was a story behind it, an incident that had driven her out here, but neither my aunt nor my mother would ever speak of it.

Abruptly, I was heaved into an embrace that was every bit as painful as it was touching. "You still shouldn't be here," Winnie muttered in my ear, then shoved me away with trembling hands.

"Maybe not."

"They'll come after you. Especially if—"

I cut her off with an upraised hand. "Don't worry about me, okay? I'm a grown man now. I can take care of myself."

Thick arms folded across an ample bosom. "Says the grown man with a shiner."

I smirked. "Ah, there's that world-famous wit. I've missed you, Winn."

She sighed and ran sausage-like fingers through her short, salt-and-pepper hair. "C'mon," she grumbled, a smile peeking through her stony visage. "Let's fix some dinner."

CHAPTER 2

October 11, 1993 ... 12:25 p.m.

W hatcha gonna do, pussy?"
Brian Whitney had me by the shirt, his mouth stretched into a menacing sneer. My jaw ached. I wanted to hit him back, yet my fists trembled at my sides, stuck there as if manacled in place. I was angry, but more than that, I was afraid. Not of being hurt, which struck me as odd. Compelling myself to throw a punch felt like committing to leap off a cliff—an irreversible decision that might somehow bring my entire life crashing down. The prospect was petrifying, even if my life was already shit. To my eternal shame, a tear crawled down my cheek.

"Oh, my God... look at him! Look at baby Shane—he's crying like a baby!"

A blur of movement and my mouth stung, then went numb.

A circle of my classmates egged Brian on—a kid with six inches and twenty pounds on me. "Hit him!" they jeered. "Beat his freak ass!"

Among them were former friends and neighbors. My gaze fell on Riley Haynes. He and Mike Owen, both a year younger than me, used to sleep over on Saturday nights. We'd stay up late playing Nintendo and poring through my parents' VHS collection for R-rated movies. The few with unabashed glimpses of the almighty female anatomy had been rewound and paused so many times, the tapes barely even played anymore.

I missed Riley and Mike. I missed having friends. I missed being just like everyone else.

Another knuckle sandwich, this one to the eye.

Other than me, only three fifth graders had survived the drowning to start school in the fall; two girls who had yet to turn ten, and a twelve-year-old boy who had already been held back twice. The girls transferred to Jay Elementary.

The boy?

Smack. Now my nose was bleeding.

Not gonna lie—the boy had one hell of a wicked jab.

With the school board in a pinch, they'd administered proficiency tests for the two of us to skip a grade. I supposed this was the path of least resistance, considering no other school wanted us. At the risk of sounding jaded, Brian Whitney was dumb as a bag of rocks. Chances are, he didn't even finish the test. And let's be honest: I wasn't exactly a genius, either. Neither of us was smart enough to fool that test, yet we both managed to squeak through. Rubber-stamped on our way as a matter of convenience over merit.

I didn't blame the school board; what else were they supposed to do?

Brian might not have been the brightest guy around, but he had something I envied: a devil-be-damned disregard for consequences.

Just hit him back! Why couldn't I do it?

Brian reared back for a kick and I surprised myself; not by throwing a punch, but by catching the kick against my side and sweeping his other leg from under him. I pounced on him, scrambling to get behind him. I snaked an arm around his neck and locked it in place.

Years later, I'd learn to refine this technique for the sake of choking out an opponent—not to literally keep him from breathing, to be clear, but to briefly cut off the blood supply to his brain. A few seconds of concentrated pressure, and nighty-night.

For the moment though, Brian was awake and kicking. "Let go of me, you freak!" he screamed.

I tightened my clench on his neck and gazed wildly up and down the hallway. Mrs. Leopold was standing in her doorway down the hall, just watching; realizing she'd been spotted, my homeroom teacher backed halfway into her classroom. She'd lost a niece in the drowning, I knew. A girl with strawberry-blonde hair named Kimberley. We used to eat lunch at the same table and talk about books. She was nice.

But none of that mattered now. Kimberley was gone. They were all gone, except for me.

Suddenly, salvation arrived. My new music teacher, Mr. Green, was quite possibly the only adult in the entire school who didn't wish me harm. I guess he didn't know any better yet. He broke up the fight and paraded Brian and me past Mrs. Leopold's classroom toward the principal's office. The woman eyed me bitterly for a second in passing, and then took a moment to appraise Mr. Green, crossing her arms.

"What's wrong with you?" he snapped.

Her expression turned to bored indignation; she took a step back and swung her door shut.

Just a few months. That's all it had taken for the whole school—the whole town, really—to turn its back on me. To forget that I was one of them. To villainize a ten-year-old boy as if he was the devil himself.

Mr. Green left me with the nurse and continued on to the office with Brian in tow. Mrs. Lamont gave me an ice pack and a handful of tissues but refused to look at me. She hadn't lost a child in the drowning; not even a distant relative. But if you commingle with a lynch mob long enough, their hate begins to feel normal. Maybe even righteous.

I waited there until the principal sent for me, doing my damnedest to keep from crying in front of Mrs. Lamont—a woman whose heart probably melted at the sight of a puppy but turned to stone at the sight of me. Her son Ricky was a high schooler and widely regarded as a bully; I sensed the same predatory instincts in her that day. The irony wasn't lost on me—that someone like her would take on the mantle of school nurse, a caregiver.

God, why hadn't I just died?

If only I could've gone back in time, I'd have found a way.

Back when I believed in God, that's precisely what I prayed for.

CHAPTER 3

July 8, 2018 ... 7:30 p.m.

I kept telling myself I was home because of my mother, to be there when her time came. But that wasn't entirely true, even if I couldn't bring myself to admit it. It was the dreams. Since the drowning, they'd been one of the few constants in my life. They didn't frighten me anymore, though I still woke in tears now and then. With the drowning anniversary fast approaching, the dreams were becoming more intense by the day. More textured and desperate, as if they were no longer dreams at all, but repressed memories clawing their way to the surface. No matter how I tried to marginalize their importance, I knew in my gut that I was supposed to be here.

I'd been summoned.

One thing was for sure: I couldn't stay with my mom. As much as I wanted to be at her side during those final days, something was coming—something ugly, as cold and unrelenting as time itself. I refused to draw it into the only place I'd ever known unconditional love. My mother's home was sacred to me. It was a sanctuary.

There were no motels close to home, so I settled for a room on the outskirts of town. The Starboard Inn wasn't a palace by any means, but I'd lived in worse with my dad. Sixty-five dollars a night. I paid for the first two in advance; we'd just have to see where things went from there.

Trudging out to unit nine, I wrinkled my nose at the rancor of weed on the breeze. Several doors down, a kid in his early twenties exited a room, shoving a baggie into his pocket on the way out. Just as he reached his car—a Honda Accord with shitty brass rims and a cheesy spoiler on the back—the kid noticed me. He hesitated with a hand on his car door, eyes bugging. I gave him an indifferent chin nod and busied myself with the task of unlocking my door.

Inside, I took a leak and brushed my teeth. The drive from St. Louis finally caught up to me as I stretched out on the bed. I fell asleep to the incessant hum of a light ballast just outside my door.

Almost immediately, the dream came.

Four men with leering grins and pistols dangling from their belts. One pushed me down, another kicked me in the stomach. A necklace cinched around my throat as a third man unzipped his pants and straddled me. The fourth hung back, his face obscured in the shadow of his hat.

"Get her good," one goaded.

This part of the dream had confused me for many years—to be referenced as a woman. In the early days, back when my naivete was still intact, I'd thought the man was going to piss on me. Now

I knew better. My skirt was torn free, exposing gangly legs the color of cinnamon. I wanted to plead for the men to stop, but for all my fear, I couldn't squeak out a word. I could barely breathe, much less speak. My fingers groped at the necklace, trying desperately to stretch a gap between the beaded strand and my frail throat.

When the man was done, he clambered to his feet, grinning and out of breath. Only then did the tension around my neck release. I sucked in blessed air and closed my legs at the knees. And then a gun barrel appeared, hovering inches over my face.

"Go on, do it."

The barrel trembled, as did I. This part of the dream was new, and all the more shocking.

"Goddammit, son—shoot her already. We got things to do."

A second of silence stretched into an eternity, broken by an annoyed snort. "Jesus, kid. Hand it here, then."

An explosion of light enveloped me.

I woke with a start, my heart bucking like a wild animal in my chest. The dream had never gone this far. I felt defiled, enraged.

It took a moment to realize that the light in my dream wasn't merely imagined. Headlights were blasting against my window, slicing between the blinds. The opening and closing of vehicle doors resounded outside, followed by the hisses of men too drunk to realize just how loud they really were.

I'd known they would come; just not this quickly.

A fist pounded on my door. I probably shouldn't have answered it—I knew what awaited me, after all—but my pride was at the reins. I wasn't afraid, anyway; I'd known real fear only moments ago, in my dream. Of course, that fear had been experienced vicariously through someone else—an elderly woman without a means of protecting herself.

I wasn't an elderly woman, and I damn sure wasn't helpless.

Opening the door, I leaned against the door jam. Cast in silhouette, five men formed a semi-circle around me. Maybe they hadn't expected me to open the door; that, or maybe they'd expected me to do so more fearfully. Whatever the case, they seemed at a loss for how to get the ball rolling with me standing there so calmly.

Five long seconds crawled by. I decided to throw them a bone. "If you're in the market for some bud, that's three doors down. Just follow your nose if you can't count that high."

This only befuddled them more.

"Okay," I chuckled through a yawn. "Might as well come on in, then."

They didn't. One finally managed to speak up, though. "You're not wanted around here, asshole."

I nodded with a tired shrug.

The man closest to the door cleared his throat. "No need for things to get ugly, Shane. We just want you to leave."

My heart ached a little. "That you, Mr. Green?" I used my hand as a visor against the headlights to get a better look at the old man. Once upon a time, he'd been kind enough to stick up for me. It seemed like a lifetime ago, but I'd be lying if I said it didn't sting like a bitch to see him now, rising against me with the likes of these douchebags.

Another voice chimed in. "Don't matter who we are. We speak for the town, and we want you gone."

I waited, my gaze bouncing around the group. When no one

else had anything to add, I sighed. "Okay. Thanks for stopping by, fellas. Now, if you don't mind, I'm gonna head back inside for some shuteye."

I was only marginally surprised when a gun was drawn. I squinted against the headlights, cocking my head. There was a time when this situation might've scared the shit out of me; it only managed to irritate me now. "Seriously?" I groaned. "What is that, a .22? You really think that little varmint popper's gonna scare anyone?"

I drew the .44 Magnum from the back of my waistband—and not a moment too soon, considering it was dragging my boxers down my ass. "Now this bad boy, here? It'll damn near take your head off." I leveled it from the waist and offered a crooked smirk.

Wisely, they backed off. But not without a demonstration of sheer redneck brilliance. The .22 popped like a cap gun. I cast a glance at my rental car; one of the tires hissed in protest. Had I sprung for damage insurance?

Pfft. Yeah, right.

"You did say you wanted me gone, right?" I needled with equal parts exasperation and amusement. "I mean, how the hell am I supposed to leave with a flat tire?"

"Goddammit, Ricky," one of them hissed. "What the hell?"

I squinted and leaned in for a closer look. "Ricky? That you, Ricky Lamont?"

"Y'all watch what yer sayin', wouldja?" grumbled another guy, this one built like a beanpole.

"Don't sweat it, Paul," I mused. "I'd recognize your voice anywhere." The man's diction was a dead ringer for Larry the Cable Guy, even if there wasn't a funny bone to be found in that puny body of his. He was destined for a life working in bait shops or plugging tires.

Not that my future was any brighter.

I raised my revolver and squeezed the trigger. The blast sent my visitors back into their truck in inelegant dives. The front end of their vehicle dropped eight inches in fractions of a second.

"There," I said reasonably. "Now we're even."

Ears ringing, I shut the door and padded back to bed. I cuddled into my blanket and tried to tune out the racket of assholes changing a truck tire.

God, I hated this town.

November 12, 1990 ... 10:15 a.m.

There were few things I despised as a child more than going to church. I didn't mind Sunday school so much—even if it was boring—but the main service was downright miserable. The banal announcements, the constant *stand up, sit down; stand up, sit down.* Singing along to monotonous hymns with fifty verses, listening to the preacher drone on and on about the same stuff, week after week. Chided for every yawn or surreptitious glance behind me. The stiffness of it all, the ritualistic tedium—they drove me up the wall.

Ugh.

I didn't realize the woman was dead when she sat down next to me. Maybe if I had, things would've turned out differently; after all, what was about to happen would set the tone for the rest of my childhood.

She was ancient—by seven-year-old standards, that is—with ashen skin that shone like wax. She wore a pearl necklace and a butterfly broach, her silver hair gathered in the bulb of a gaudy summer hat. The woman stared straight ahead through the entire sermon, still as a marble bust.

Then the organ kicked in and out came the hymnals again. The offering plate worked its way down the rows.

Bringing in the sheaves, bringing in the sheaves;
We will come rejoicing, bringing in the sheaves.

When the offering plate reached me, I tried to pass it along to the woman, but her gaze remained fixed ahead, oblivious.

Sowing in the sunshine, sowing in the shadows;
Fearing neither clouds nor winter's chilling breeze—

An usher cleared his throat impatiently at the end of the row.

"Excuse me," I whispered to the woman.

My mom pinched my elbow, but by then, the usher had crab-stepped down the row to snatch the plate away.

Bringing in the sheaves, bringing in the sheaves;
We will come rejoicing, bringing in the—

Abruptly, the woman turned to look at me. Her eyes were dull and indistinct, irises feathering into a jaundiced murk of broken blood vessels. Her mouth dropped open and I thought she might speak; but instead, her lips stretched wider and wider until her lower jaw popped free, hinging inside out to show off a torn gray tongue and half a dozen nubs of broken teeth. She leaned toward me with claw-like fingers spread wide before her, her mouth impossibly

23

huge, and honest to God, I thought she was about to swallow me.

At the precise moment when the music finally stopped, the sanctuary resounded with my gut-splitting scream. I reached for the protection of my mother's arms. "Don't let her eat me!" I cried.

While the congregation whispered and snickered, and my mother hid her face in mortification, the woman rose and strode clumsily down the aisle to the front of the church. Mere feet from the preacher, who looked in my direction with a nervous frown, she dropped to her knees and… and then she was gone.

I'd never live this incident down. It tainted the very fabric of my adolescence, ushering in an endless supply of ridicule and alienation that I doubted would ever fade. Yet there's no denying a faint, silver lining to it all; after all, my mom never brought me to church again.

July 9, 2018 … 8:07 a.m.

I got the phone call a little after eight the next morning. Outside, the sun inched up the horizon, setting the motel's cheap miniblinds aglow. I heard the words clearly enough, even if Winnie bellowed them through ratcheting sobs. When my aunt ran out of steam, she blew her nose and fell silent.

It surprised me how easily the platitudes sprang to mind.
Her suffering is finally over.
She'll always be with us in spirit.

"She's in a better place now," I said finally with an air of certainty that I didn't actually feel.

"Yes, she is," Winnie agreed.

I raised the blinds to let the morning sun wash over me. "So what do we do now?" I had to ask.

"Your mom didn't want any kind of service."

"Why not?"

My aunt was silent for a moment. "Do you really have to ask?"

I supposed I didn't.

"She wanted to be cremated," Winnie said faintly. "She told me that much."

Cremated. Somehow the idea felt sacrilegious, if not merely taboo. "What about her ashes?"

Winnie grunted in the back of her throat. "She didn't say. I don't think she cared, Shane. I think she just wanted to go without a bunch of fuss."

The notion brought tears to my eyes. This was the real tragedy—that my sweet mother had dragged a mountain of unearned guilt right into her deathbed. She deserved better than that. God knows her image had been besmirched enough in life because of me. Was it really so much to ask for her to depart this world with a little dignity?

"Listen," I sniffled. "I'll head your way shortly. I'd like to see her."

"Okay. Talk to you soon."

It took ten minutes to change the tire. When I was done, I sifted through the glovebox for a copy of my rental agreement. As feared, I had indeed foregone the extra damage liability insurance.

Ah, the price of being a rebel.

Winnie was waiting at the end of the driveway when I arrived. I gave her an awkward hug and we headed inside. I tried not to look around; every knickknack and framed photo seemed to reach out for me, demanding to be acknowledged. Yet, there was a stillness about the place that I'd never experienced before; twelve-hundred square feet of utter emptiness, despite a lifetime's accumulation of useless stuff.

Winnie stayed in the kitchen while I headed down the hallway. My mother was lying on her side with her back to the bedroom door. If I didn't know better, I might've assumed she was sleeping. I rounded the bed with hands trembling and dropped to my knees.

"Oh, Mom," I sighed. Her eyes were closed, her mouth slightly agape. Silver hair was draped in a limp pile against the pillow. I laid a hand on her cheek; her skin was unnaturally cool and stiff to the touch. Fighting off tears, I nearly overlooked what was in her hand—something looped around her fingers in neat rows.

It came loose with a gentle tug, uncoiling under tension as if it was a living thing. Entranced, I sat on the edge of the bed. My pulse picked up its pace as I ran my fingers over the beads—yellow-tinted ovals carved from bone and threaded on a thick strand of leather.

No, it can't be…

But it was. The necklace from my dream. I'd fought against it in my sleep more times than I could count; by touch alone, I recognized it without the slightest doubt.

Suddenly, Winnie shrieked from the doorway. The sound startled me to my feet; my aunt's eyes were wide and more frightened than I'd ever seen them. I took a step toward her, reaching out a reassuring hand.

It was then that I realized what she was looking at. It wasn't the necklace, but my mother—a dead woman who was somehow sitting upright, her now-milky eyes gazing at me, unseeing. From her mouth, something black protruded. She spat and it flew in a lazy arch to the floor.

"You said she was dead, Winnie!" I snapped, clambering back to my mother's side. Her gaze lingered toward the end of the bed, where I'd been standing only a moment ago. "It's okay, Mom. Everything's okay."

I laid a hand on her shoulder, giving her a gentle push. "C'mon, let's lay back down." To Winnie, I hissed, "Get her some water, would you?"

My aunt remained frozen in place.

I let my attention return to my mother. She was on her side again, just as I'd found her when I arrived. I checked her pulse and found none.

"Jesus," I hissed through clenched teeth.

My conversation with Winnie shortly thereafter wasn't a pleasant one. I was angry and confused, and rightfully so. For Winnie's part, she couldn't bring herself to admit even the possibility of being mistaken. Neither could she be coaxed back inside. She stood in the grass some thirty feet from the side door and shook her head adamantly. Though annoyed, I followed her outside.

"She was dead, Shane," Winnie wailed, her face round and shiny in the morning sun. "I-I'm telling you. Dead as a goddamn doornail!"

I rubbed the bridge of my nose; still a little tender from a recent break, courtesy of an overzealous sparring partner back in St. Louis. "You checked her pulse?"

Winnie's expression darkened. "Of course I did, smartass. She wasn't breathing, either." She bit off an angry sob and stamped her foot.

I gritted my teeth, doing my best to hold it together. In through the nose, out through the mouth. Slow and steady.

Repeat.

She'd seemed dead to me too, if I was being honest. "I guess it doesn't really matter, does it?" I pointed out. "Either way, she's gone now."

Winnie wiped her eyes and headed to her RV without another word. Her door slammed shut just as a car ambled up the driveway.

I almost didn't recognize the preacher when I answered the door; he'd gained weight over the years, which softened his features. Tan and bespectacled, he wore a tidy moustache.

"Reverend," I said in greeting.

"Well, my goodness, Shane. You sure have grown!"

It was tempting to point out that he had as well, but it seemed a little rude. Maybe later. "I'm guessing Winnie called you?"

His eyebrows shot up. "Well, that would be a first."

"Never mind. Come on in."

I put on a pot of coffee, amazed that despite the many years I'd been gone, everything remained exactly as I remembered it.

Not only were the coffee mugs precisely where I expected them to be, the mugs themselves were each familiar. The sugar cannister, the cream—I knew exactly where to find them without a fleeting thought.

I'm not sure why this affected me so profoundly, but it did. As the coffee maker burbled away, I leaned against the counter and fought to keep my composure.

"Is she sleeping, your mother?" the reverend asked. "I know the medicine makes her drowsy. Especially the pain pills."

I clenched my teeth and took a deep breath. I turned to him with trembling hands. "She's gone, Reverend."

The man's head cocked slightly, his eyes turning inquisitive. "Beg your pardon?"

I swallowed.

"Oh, no," he whispered. His expression grew taut, strained. "She didn't look good yesterday, but I…" He trailed off, then cleared his throat. "My goodness. When?"

"Just a few minutes ago."

He took a step toward me and planted a hand on my shoulder, squeezing gently. "Oh, Shane. I'm so very sorry."

I could only nod in reply. The coffee maker slurped from the counter, the pot now full.

"You know, I was about your age when I lost my mother," the reverend said. "Car accident." He shook his head with a melancholy frown. "Even after all these years, it still seems like yesterday. When someone we care for passes from this life to the next, it's normal for us to feel—"

As the reverend prattled on, I couldn't help but think of the last time I'd stepped foot in his church. The dead woman with the funny hat. A thought struck me—one I would've kept to myself in a better state of mind.

"Did she wear a butterfly broach?" I asked, almost unaware that I'd spoken.

The reverend's lips froze in midsentence and his fatherly smile curled. "I'm sorry, did you say—"

"Your mom—did she own a butterfly broach? Yellow with red spots on the wings?"

The man's cheeks bloomed pink. Five long seconds ticked by while he stared at me without a word. Almost entranced, I filled a mug with coffee.

"She had a big sunhat too, right? With little flowers?"

When I went to fill a second, the reverend finally spoke. "I think, uh... I should probably get going, Shane. I'll give Winnie a call to, uh... you know. Discuss funeral arrangements."

I turned back to him with the coffee pot still in hand.

"So sorry for your loss," he added, his eyes unable to meet mine.

Seconds later, he was backing down the driveway—much faster than he'd driven up it, incidentally. Poor guy. That'll teach him to look after his flock.

I sipped my coffee and scowled. "Nice one, asshole," I mumbled to myself.

My gaze crawled toward the hallway, where a sliver of my mother's doorway was just visible. My mom was in there. No... not my mom. A body of inanimate flesh that had once given birth to me. The rest was gone.

At once, the air seemed to thicken. Try as I might, I couldn't catch a decent breath. I needed to get out of there. I pushed outside in tears, stumbling to my car like a mad man.

To my absolute delight, the Starboard Inn welcomed my return with a broken air conditioner. I called the office and left a voicemail when no one picked up. The room wasn't sweltering yet, but it would be soon enough. My phone buzzed from my pocket. A text from Adam, my sparring partner.

Are you ever coming back? Running out of dudes to beat on.

I tapped out an ambiguous response and shoved the phone back in my pocket. I fell into bed, dazed. Numb inside, detached in a way that was becoming all too familiar. The popcorn ceiling was stained here and there, I couldn't help but notice, with cobwebs thick at the corners. How many leaks had this shithole sustained over the years? How many sad, pathetic souls—counting mine—had rested their weary heads on this worn out bed? Too many to count.

My cell phone came to life. I slipped it from my pocket and answered without a glance at the screen.

"Hey," I mumbled, feeling half a second behind the word.

"I'm sorry, Shane."

It took a long moment to string together who was sorry, and what she was sorry about, but I managed to catch up. "It's fine, Winnie. I'm sorry, too. Did the reverend get hold of you?"

"He left me a message."

"You gonna call him back?"

A husky chuckle. "Prob'ly not." She was quiet for a few seconds. "Anyway, the funeral home's sendin' someone for her."

The image of a stranger zipping my mother into a plastic bag and heaving her onto a gurney like a piece of meat stole my breath for a second. I closed my eyes and took a deep, cathartic breath. "Okay," I croaked.

"Listen, how long are you stickin' around?"

The question caught me off guard because I hadn't given the subject much thought. The numbness faded a bit and I sat up. Squinting toward the broken AC, I bit off a sigh of irritation. "For a while, I guess."

Winnie swallowed audibly. "You sure? Don't you have a job to get back to? An apartment or sumthin?"

I did, of course. But they were expendable. "Nothing that can't wait."

She cleared her throat, sniffled. "Thank God," she muttered.

"We'll talk again soon, okay?"

My aunt exhaled long and hard between her teeth. "Okay. But do me a favor though, would you?"

I peeked through the blinds at the parking lot and watched a stray dog trot by. "What's that?"

"Try to keep a low profile. Stay out of town if you can help it."

"I will," I promised, and let the miniblind slats fall back in place. "But not today. There's something I need to do."

She grunted. "Uh-huh."

"Give me a break, Winn. I'm not here to stir up trouble."

She laughed humorlessly. "We both know trouble comes and goes as it pleases with you, Shane."

My gaze traveled to the revolver on my nightstand. "Yeah, I hear you. I'm gonna go now, okay? I need to pay someone a visit."

She didn't bother with a follow-up question; she knew perfectly well who I had in mind. The moment I disconnected, my phone pulsed again. I answered the call and headed for the car.

"Mr. Gibson?"

"That's me."

"This is Katie Quinn with Winthroe Classic Insurance. I'm calling regarding your vehicle claim?"

"Sure. What's up?"

"This is just a courtesy call to inform you the claim has been processed. You can expect a check for the full value of your policy sometime in the next few weeks."

"That's great," I sighed. "Can you confirm the amount for me?"

A clacking of keys. "Looks like forty-six thousand."

Thank God...

"Your policy will also reimburse the cost of a rental for up to thirty days. Just keep your receipts."

This wasn't news, but it didn't hurt to hear it reaffirmed.

I wrapped up the call with a promise to complete a survey about my customer experience once it arrived in the mail.

Mm-hmm. Like that was gonna happen.

I threw the car into gear and put the Starboard Inn in my rearview mirror. Five minutes later, I pulled into the parking lot of Mo's Cafe. I hesitated in the car with my hand on the door latch. It was selfish of me, coming here—I knew that perfectly well. Nevertheless, before I could change my mind, I exited the car and headed inside.

A woman in her late fifties stiffened behind the register as I walked in. An elderly gentleman stood by with a twenty between knobby fingers, but the woman remained frozen in place, her mouth slightly agape.

"Hey, Barbara," I mumbled.

She swallowed and turned her attention back to the man. She made change and gave him a fleeting smile. Her eyes flicked back to me. "Sit wherever you want," she said, though her prickly expression had something entirely different to say.

"Is she here?" I asked.

The woman shook her head, jiggling a blob of bangs several decades out of style. "She don't work here no more."

I'd figured as much. "Any idea where I can find her?"

Barbara gave me her back and wiped a nearby table clean. "You oughta leave her be, Shane. She's doing good for once."

"You make it sound like I'm a bad influence."

"Far as I'm concerned, you are."

I gave her backside a resentful frown. "I don't do drugs, you know. Never have."

"Don't matter. Last time you came around, Mindy was real happy to see you. Then you just up and left, and she disappeared for a week. Lost her job here, ended up in rehab again."

I closed my eyes. "I'm sorry to hear that. But in fairness, I didn't just *up and leave.* I came here for a visit and went home when it was over." To be more precise, the sheriff invited me to leave. Damn near at gunpoint.

"If you say so."

"I do. And either way, that was an awful long time ago."

Barbara turned with a bit of steel in her eyes. "Sure was. But you just can't seem to leave her alone, can you?" She opened her mouth to add something, but clamped it shut without another word. She busied herself with the task of laying out napkins and silverware.

I took a deep breath and released it slowly. "You ever been in love, Barbara? I mean, absolutely sick in love?"

The weathered waitress peeked over her shoulder. "Who hasn't?"

"If you truly had, you'd know that it never really goes away. You can't turn it off like a switch. It stays with you always. At best, you learn to bury it."

"There's a word for that, you know, and it ain't love. It's called obsession."

Maybe she was right; I'd never thought about it in those terms.

"Don't matter now, anyway," Barbara was saying. "Whatever you two had together? That's long gone, Shane. She's a different person. She ain't perfect, but she deserves better than…"

"Better than me," I finished for her.

She looked away to tidy up her silverware arrangement, but a subtle shrug gave me all the confirmation I needed.

My cheeks flushed. With the death of my mother still fresh, my emotions got the better of me. I was tired of this shit. The cold shoulder, the silent treatment. "What did I ever do?" I demanded. "To you, or anyone else in this goddamn town?"

Barbara stood straight with her back still to me. I caught a long glimpse of her reflection in the booth window. She hadn't aged well. "Ain't nuthin you did, Shane. It's who you are. *What* you are. You oughta know that by now."

I did, and that was the problem. I hadn't done a damn thing to anyone, yet I would always be despised here. And for reasons that I couldn't quite grasp, this shit town still managed to draw me back, time and time again.

CHAPTER 4

Back at my rental car—a sexless sedan without so much as a brand decal to betray it's make or model—I found an envelope pinned between my windshield and a wiper blade. A quick glance around found no one loitering nearby. A car passed in one direction, three more in the other.

In the privacy of the driver's seat, I tore into the envelope. I expected a hate letter of some kind—*Get out while you still can, shit for brains!*—but instead, the envelope contained a photograph. My blood ran cold at the sight of it. It was an old Polaroid, its edges yellow and curled. I let my finger wander across the surface, trembling. The men from my dreams—here they were. Three of the four, anyway; immortalized in sepia tones, posed with some kind of plaque between them against a backdrop of trees and a cloudless sky. On the bottom margin, a caption had been scrawled long ago in careful strokes.

Ralph Crowley and friends, 1968.

The hairs on my arms stood on end. *1968.* Twenty-five years before the drowning. Something had happened back then, I knew. Something terrible that no one dared to talk about, but everyone acknowledged.

Ralph Crowley. The name was familiar; I looked it up on my phone and found him immediately. Tossing the photo onto the passenger seat, I started the engine.

I parked at a convenience store with a view of the car lot across the road. Crowley's Fine Auto Sales. The newest vehicle in the line-up was easily five years old. There, a man in his seventies or eighties hobbled between SUVs behind a young couple. It was him—the first man in the picture. I'd need a closer look to be sure, but I had little doubt.

The question was, what was I supposed to do about it?

I approached the car lot on foot, leaving my car at the convenience store. The young couple was piling into their dated minivan by then, muttering the obligatory 'thanks, we'll give it some thought' on their way out. Crowley waved them off as if to bid them good riddance.

"They don't make it easy, do they?" I remarked with a plastic smile, trying to play it cool.

"Hell no. They never do." He flashed his own plastic smile—a bit more practiced and therefore more refined, I couldn't help but notice—but then gave me the once over and froze. "Hey, I know you."

My smile fell away. "Nah, I don't think so."

His upper lip wrinkled in disgust. "You're that damn Gibson kid."

My temper cracked its knuckles. "Knowing my name isn't the same as knowing me." I leaned forward, breaching the respectable boundaries of his personal space by several inches. "You don't know a damn thing about me. Only what you've heard."

If he was intimidated at all, he hid it well. "I knew your daddy well enough. He was a weirdo, just like you."

"My dad was bipolar. What's your excuse?"

"Excuse for what?"

"Well, you're the one stuck here, lording over used cars all by your lonesome."

So much for playing it cool.

"Listen here, you little shit. Wanna buy a car? I'll set you up with a fine set of wheels. Just add a grand to the sticker price. Otherwise, get the hell outa here."

"Will do, old timer. Real quick, though—" I flashed him the photograph. "—that's you, right?"

He opened his mouth in surprise, but I cut off any response.

"Now, you're easy enough to recognize with those monkey ears, but these other guys? They don't look so familiar."

"Where'd you get that?" the old man whispered.

"They friends of yours? Locals?"

"I'm serious, kid. Where'd you get that?" He made a clumsy grab for it, but I stepped easily out of range.

"Tell you what, I'll make a deal with you," I offered reasonably. "Tell me what happened back in '68, and the picture's all yours."

A sickly wave of uncertainty rippled across his face, replaced at once by something far more sinister. Some guys, they're so full of bad mojo it leaks from their pores. Crowley was like that, I realized. The kind of guy you steered clear of if you had a choice, and that was saying the very least.

"Get the hell out of here, kid," he hissed. "Don't make me call the cops."

I left the old man to glower over his crappy cars and drove two blocks over. Completely unrelated to Crowley, I'd experienced an epiphany; where did one go for information when all else failed?

Why, the library, of course.

The Langley Public Library might've been the quietest place in town. Which was a shame, if you asked me, because I could've moved right in. It was small, but cozy and pleasantly familiar. I'd spent a lot of time here as an adolescent. I can remember curling up to read for hours at a time, not once feeling that I'd wasted a minute.

There was only one person on duty—a woman my age with a crewcut and baggy khakis.

"Jean?" I hissed with a grin. "Jean 'the Mean Machine' Keller? Is that you?"

Her eyes widened, taking me in. "Shane?"

"The one and only." I swooped in and wrapped her in a bear hug. "How the hell are you?"

Jean laughed and clapped me on the back. "Doing well, doing well." She stepped back to give me a long, appraising glance. "You look good. Except for the shiner."

"So do you."

She grimaced. "You're a damn liar."

"Hey, not everyone can rock a crewcut. You pull it off better than most."

She chuckled. "Always the charmer, Shane. It's no wonder Mindy fell so hard for you."

The comment knocked me off balance. I tried not to flinch, to regain my equilibrium. At a momentary loss for words, I dragged the photograph from my back pocket and handed it over.

"Well, would you look at that. Hard to miss Mr. Crowley, that's for sure. And Mr. Middleton, too."

"As in, Middleton Construction?"

"Yep."

"Which one's he?"

Jean tapped a finger on the man in the middle. "Raymond Middleton. He's in his nineties now. Cranky old bastard, I'm tellin' you."

"He's still alive?"

"Far as I know. Living the dream at the Crossroads Nursing Home, last I heard. Not sure about this other guy. Looks a little familiar, but…" She shook her head. "Can't quite place him. I wonder what that plaque says."

"Yeah, me too. I was thinking, do you guys keep old newspapers?"

Jean frowned. "What, like The Tribune? We try, I guess. Had a nasty flood a few years back, though. Must've lost fifteen years of history in a single day."

"What about on microfiche?"

She shrugged. "We've got a machine, but it was broken when I hired on. Frankly, you're the first person to ask about it in more than a decade. Everything's digitized these days."

"Okay, old school it is."

She nodded with a hint of apology. "What exactly are you looking for?"

"A way to identify this guy." I flicked the photo for emphasis.

The woman scrutinized me. "Okay... so what's the significance?"

"Could be nothing. Could be the key to decoding evolution."

"Smartass."

"Mm-hmm. We both know that shoe fits." My smile slipped a little. "Honestly, I'm not sure what it's all about. I'm just curious, I guess."

"Gotta say, Shane—you're not very helpful."

I crossed my arms defensively. "Hey, you're the librarian. You should be used this kind of treatment."

She guffawed. "You have no idea. Yesterday a man asked for help downloading porn on one of our computers. Brought a flash drive and everything. He called me a prude when I refused."

"Did you at least offer to show him your Playboy collection?"

"What, like my personal stash? Hell no."

I tsk-tsked with disapproval. "Prude."

"I've been called worse. Let's see what we can dig up, shall we?"

I followed Jean into the basement, where dozens of metal shelves crammed the space from wall to wall. "The newspapers are over here," she said, gesturing to the shelf nearest the door.

Upstairs, a voice called out, "Hello?"

Jean sighed. "I wish I could stay and help, but…" she nodded up the stairs. "Well, I'm short-handed today."

"No problem, I'm good."

I dug in, sifting through the boxes with single-minded determination. An hour in, I hit pay dirt in one of 1968's July issues of the Tribune. A photo similar to the one left on my windshield—this one zoomed in a bit with better lighting and a different background—accompanied an article about the city council's new funding oversight committee. A quick scan of the text revealed nothing of immediate interest, but the photo's caption was another story.

Lifelong friends Raymond Middleton and Alan Proctor congratulate Langley's newest city councilman, Ralph Crowley.

I took the stairs two at a time and slapped the paper on Jean's desk. She snatched it up with a conspiratorial smirk. "Alan Proctor," she murmured, eyes skimming the caption. "Doesn't ring a bell."

I googled the name on my phone. "Looks like he was the sheriff of Mayes county from 1963 to 1995."

Jean frowned. "So we're looking at a former sheriff, the owner of a major construction company and a former city councilman."

"Kind of makes you wonder," I muttered thoughtfully.

"It does. Is it physically possible to find a shadier bunch of guys?"

My eyebrows lifted. "That too, now that you mention it. But I was thinking along the lines of who took the picture."

"The Tribune photographer seems like a safe guess."

"Not that one," I clarified. I waved the Polaroid from my windshield. "This one. I think it was taken the same day. Look, they're all wearing the same clothes."

The librarian sucked on her lower lip. "Hmm. Good observation. Your guess is as good as mine, though."

Damn.

"You know," Jean said, "there was a lot of controversy surrounding the dam back then."

"Oh yeah? What about?"

"Well, if my grandparents were to be believed, there were some rampant good-old-boy deals happening behind the scenes. Padded maintenance contracts, embezzlement, unlawful confiscation of private property—that sort of thing. When Middleton got the maintenance contract, his family became one of the wealthiest in the county almost overnight."

"What does that have to do with Ralph Crowley and Alan Proctor?"

Jean showed me her palms. "Hell if I know. Sounds like they were buddies. Maybe that's all there is to it."

Surely not. There had to be more to it.

From nowhere, a wave of exhaustion threatened to swallow me whole. My shoulders sagged an inch or two, my eyes drooped. I should've been relieved, if not excited—I had names to match three of the four figures from my dream, after all—yet if anything, I felt even more dismayed.

"You okay, Shane?"

I bobble-headed a yes-and-no.

Jean put a hand on my shoulder. "It's the anniversary, right? Coming up next week?"

Shit. Pile that on, too. "Yeah."

"Don't take this the wrong way, Shane, but you should prob'ly make yourself scarce. People are really on edge lately"

I nodded. "They blame me."

"No, I wouldn't say that. It's more like you're…" She trailed off, stroking her chin.

"What, a bad omen?"

Jean rolled her lips, then offered a sour frown. "Yeah, I guess that fits." She sighed through her nose, her head swaying sadly. "They aren't bad people, you know. They're just superstitious. And scared."

"I know," I said. And honestly, I did. More than anything else, my cavalier distaste for the town likely stemmed from a childish need to dislike anyone who disliked me first. With a few exceptions, of course.

"Just be careful around town, will you? Even good people do stupid things when they're afraid."

"Don't worry about me. I can take care of myself."

She gave my shoulder a squeeze and let her hand drop away. "Famous last words, my friend."

"Probably so."

We fell into silence.

"How about I make a copy of the article for you?" Jean offered.

"Sure. Thanks."

She strode to a copy machine the size of a Fiat and positioned the newspaper carefully on the glass. "You know, I always hated how everyone treated you," she remarked.

The copy machine whirred to life.

I gave her a sidelong glance. "Like they treated you well?"

She shrugged. "Yeah, but I'm gay."

"So?"

"So, I didn't get half the shit you did, and I was the one challenging social norms. You were kind and smart, and fun to be around. If things had played out differently, you might've been—"

"Shit happens, Jean. Life isn't fair."

She nodded, eyes flashing with emotion. "I remember, you know."

I knew exactly what she was talking about, even if I didn't want to acknowledge it. I closed my eyes, both to hide my emotion and to spare myself the sight of hers.

"It's a gift, Shane. You realize that, don't you?"

"Gifts don't come with strings attached," I replied, a little surprised by the heat in my voice.

Jean and I had been inseparable as kindergarteners. One spring evening, while playing Uno with her parents, an old man strode through the house like he owned the place; I remember the way he glared at me, like I was a stain on his carpet. When I asked about him, Jean's parents sent me home. As for Jean, she didn't speak to me for a solid week. Guess she forgot about that part.

Some gift.

That was the summer when I first realized I wasn't like everyone else. I'd spend the better part of a decade trying to keep a lid on just how different I really was, to no avail.

For reasons that I might never understand, the dead gravitated toward me as a child. They didn't appear to seek me out intentionally, and I can assure you that I never once invited their attention. Nevertheless, they came and went, and I couldn't do a damn thing about it.

After the church incident, my parents put me on meds. The pills didn't do much, other than bubble-wrap me in a haze of indifference. I think it was actually a good poker face that finally got me off the hook. If you ignore the dead long enough, I learned, they eventually move on. As for the kids at school—the whole town, for that matter—they never looked at me the same once the rumors grew legs. Even if the drowning had never happened, I was damaged goods.

But the drowning *did* happen. And the sole survivor was the weirdo kid who saw dead people. Ghost Boy. Jean was wrong; I never stood a chance here. I was doomed from the start.

Jean was staring at me. "Do you still…"

"Nah," I said. "Not since I left with my dad." This wasn't entirely true, considering the persistence of my dreams, but it was close enough.

Jean sighed, handing over a copy of the article. "You know, it's not as uncommon as you might think, Shane. I saw a documentary—"

I felt my pulse surge, my jaw clamp shut. All at once, this was too much. "Gotta go, Jean. Thanks for your help."

"Wait, Shane. I'm sorry, I didn't—"

"No worries," I called over my shoulder. "Running a little late for an errand, that's all."

Seconds later, I was back at my car. I had the door half open when Jean hollered after me.

"Don't go pestering the sheriff, Shane!" she called through the bullhorn of a cupped hand. "That man hates you more than most!"

Didn't I know it.

CHAPTER 5

July 15, 1993 ... 4:35 p.m.

"Tell us what you did, Shane."

"I didn't do anything," I whimpered. I was tired and scared. My leg throbbed, my feet ached.

Deputy Thompson tried to keep a neutral expression, but his eyes were dark and desperate. He'd just lost a daughter, after all. "We've got witnesses, you little shit. Your buddy Mike Owen? He's already told us everything. We just need to hear it from you. In your own words."

My heart lurched. Why would Mike tell lies about me? He was supposed to my best friend. I would never lie about him. Fresh tears flowed down my cheeks. "I want my mom and dad!" I wailed. "I wanna go home!"

Another deputy, a stone-faced man who'd been idling in the

corner until now, strode to the table and crouched so that we were eye to eye. He hadn't introduced himself, but he wore a nametag. Deputy Lloyd Spence. "The faster you tell us the truth, Shane," he was saying, "the faster we can get you back home. You must be exhausted. Hungry too, I'm guessing."

I'd been in this room for what seemed like days, barefoot and dressed in pajamas. I was indeed exhausted, and hungry. More than anything though, I needed to pee. They'd given me a Coke upon arrival, and I'd been dumb enough to drink it.

"I gotta go to the bathroom really bad," I pleaded. Again.

"I know, I know. Just a few more minutes." The deputy smiled patiently, which stretched a scar on his upper lip until it turned white. "Now let's go through it one more time. You were walking down to the lake, and then what happened?"

My gaze dropped to Deputy Thompson's boots. They were caked in brackish lake mud. I thought about Carrie. Was she really dead? How could that be true? How could any of this—

"Eyes up here, Shane," the deputy snipped. "You were walking down to the lake…"

"I-I told you, I don't know. I… I don't remember. I just—"

"You just woke up in the grass near the boat ramp," he finished for me. "We've heard that already, but I wanna know what you were doing down there, Shane. What made you walk all the way to Yonker's in the first place?"

He had a point, of course; the marina was miles from home. But I could only shrug and tremble.

My last memory before waking that morning was brushing my teeth for bed and slipping under my covers. I woke on the ground, shivering, covered in dew. I remember trying to get to my feet and yelping in pain. My legs were entangled in an abandoned trotline with a series of treble hooks embedded up the length of one calf. The sun was peeking over the treetops, bruising the sky. It was eerily peaceful that morning, songbirds and insects greeting the new day as if all was well. I was crying by then, but quietly—the way my dad taught me. A shuffling came from the wet grass behind me—probably a squirrel, a rabbit—and then went still.

That's when the wailing began. First, a woman's lone voice down the shoreline a ways, followed a second later by a man's. Moment by moment, more cries crowded the spectrum of sound until the air itself was a wall of screams.

I'd explained this to the deputies too many times to count. But it wasn't what they wanted to hear. It wasn't what anyone wanted to hear. Children were dead. Someone needed to pay.

My parents got a lawyer. I don't know how they paid him, not to this day. I'd been in custody for more than ten hours by the time he showed up. The sheriff—a rail-thin man with a hat that seemed to smudge his features—popped in. Deputy Thompson glared openly at the man but looked away in the end. Something about the sheriff unsettled me even more than I already was. My eyes swiveled to the floor to escape his gaze, noticing with detached curiosity that his bootlaces didn't match. One was black, the other brown.

"Let's go," he said.

Wordlessly, the sheriff and his deputies left me in that little room while they hashed things out with the lawyer in the hallway. I don't know how long they were out there; I could hear them arguing for what seemed like forever. Eventually though, the door opened a crack and the face of a complete stranger poked inside.

"C'mon, Shane," he said in a soothing, fatherly tone. "Let's get out of here."

I hesitated with tear-stained cheeks.

"It's okay, bud. My name's Jonathan Caldwell. I'm your lawyer, and I'm here to take you home."

I stood on the legs of a newborn fawn, weak and tremulous. I saw the man's gaze slide downward, followed by an abrupt shift in his demeanor. A wave of humiliation crashed over me.

"I-I'm sorry," I mewled in shame. "I-I tried to hold it."

CHAPTER 6

July 9, 2018 ... 2:30 p.m.

Mindy Thompson was a few years my senior. Seemed like a big deal, back when we were kids. As adults, it amounted to nothing. There were far more significant wedges between us now, anyway.

When I pulled against the curb in front of her parents' house, I had one of those irrational premonitions—the kind you recognize intellectually as unlikely, even if you go rigid at the thought. Sheriff Thompson would answer the door with a shotgun; he'd tip his Stetson and blast a hole through my chest.

Well, so be it.

The door opened before I could knock. The woman standing there wasn't Mindy; she was an older, weary-faced version of the woman with thinning hair and skin like cracked porcelain.

"She ain't here, Shane." Her voice was firm, but kind.

"Yeah," I sighed. "I figured it was a longshot. Had to try, though."

"Come on in," she said warmly. "Let's chat."

She didn't have to twist my arm; I'd take kindness wherever I could find it in this town. I followed her inside, past a wall of family photos; the images were too numerous and disarrayed to think of as anything but a shrine. I tried to be strong—to keep my gaze trained ahead—but I couldn't help myself.

Images of Mindy—the girl I'd fallen for as a kid and had yet to move on from—stung like salt in a nasty paper cut, yet those I could bear; it was the pictures of Mindy's little sister that truly gutted me. Sweet Carrie Thompson, with a smile that could've powered the whole town.

"It's almost her anniversary, you know," Mrs. Thompson observed in a voice that rasped like linen against concrete. "Twenty-five years. Long years." Her eyes glazed over. "You'd think the pain woulda faded by now."

"It never fades," I replied, resenting the waver in my voice. My weakness. Swallowing a mouthful of desert sand, I tried to shake off my emotion. "You just… acclimate to it. Like freezing water."

The old woman grunted in agreement and continued on to the kitchen. I stole a parting glance at one more picture—this one of Mindy in her high school cap and gown—and then left the living room behind, bruised and bleeding and trying for all I was worth to keep it together.

Mrs. Thompson poured coffee and offered me a cookie from a tin. I declined the latter.

"How's the sheriff?" I dared to ask.

Eyes darkening, Mrs. Thompson shook her head. "Wouldn't know. Divorced him three years ago. Last I heard, he bought a few acres in Pryor." She cocked her head. "You didn't know?"

"No, I didn't."

Her lips pursed. "Took some real guts to knock on that door, then."

I smiled. "Yeah, well. I don't scare as easily as I used to."

Her gaze settled on the fading bruise under my eye. "I'll bet. I heard about your mom, Shane. I'm so sorry for your loss."

I nodded my thanks.

"I went to see her last week, you know. With my church prayer group."

My eyebrows shot up.

"We had a good talk. She seemed at peace. Said she was ready to greet the Lord."

Nodding dumbly, I took a sip from my coffee. It was weak with a burnt undertone, what Winnie would've referred to as *Baptist brew*.

A long silence crept in, and I felt compelled to break it. "Sorry to hear about your divorce," I offered.

Mrs. Thompson's eyes rolled with amusement, accentuated by a wide grin. "Like hell you are!"

I offered a laughing grimace. "Cut me some slack, would you? I'm trying to be polite."

As her laugh trailed off, the old woman's smile turned wistful. "I was only seventeen when we met, you know. I was already engaged. But Jim… he just came along and swept me off my feet."

I could easily picture the man sweeping people off their feet, but in a very different way; perhaps with a baseball bat or a nice cattle prod. A bloody machete, if the mood was right.

Mrs. Thompson chuckled to herself, savoring memories long past. "Yes, he was a good man."

"You say that like he's dead."

"Might as well be. Losing Carrie…" Mrs. Thompson wheezed a melancholy sigh. "It changed him."

She didn't have to tell me that. I'll never forget the hate in his eyes as I limped from that interrogation room with my lawyer. If he could've murdered me then and there, he would have.

"Actually," she muttered, "I think he was already half gone by then. I s'pose I just noticed it more after Carrie died."

I nodded, unsure of what to say.

"I suggest you steer clear of him, Shane," she warned, sweeping a few cookie crumbs from the table with the edge of her hand. "He ain't a man to be trifled with."

I tried for a reassuring smile, but I could feel it fall flat. "It must've been a big adjustment, Mrs. Thompson," I remarked. "Living alone after so many years."

"It's Alice, now. Just… Alice."

"Okay. Alice."

"Anyway, life after divorce ain't as bad as you might imagine. Jim's always been a man with unreasonable standards and a short fuse. In some ways, it's like I can breathe for the first time. And I've never minded time alone. I like the quiet."

Mrs. Thompson—Alice—coughed into a bony fist and slurped her coffee. "So."

I brought the mug to my lips again and took a courtesy sip.

"So."

"Don't be coy, Shane," Alice needled. "Let's talk about why you're really here."

My cheeks burned. "Fair enough. How is she?"

"Oh, she has her ups and downs."

I nodded.

"She's been clean for almost a year. So she says, anyway. Got herself an apartment in town with a roommate."

"You two still close?"

A melancholy shrug. "We talk a couple times a week. I take what I can get."

I closed my eyes and pictured Mindy at the table with Carrie and me—this very table, where we'd all played Monopoly and sipped hot chocolate as kids. Carrie's unicorn footy pajamas, Mindy's budding womanhood. Everything beautiful and innocent from my childhood seemed to have centered on this table. Now it was just... a table. The finish scratched, worn through here and there, but otherwise fully functional. It didn't seem fair, though I couldn't put my finger on why.

"Grief will eat you alive, if you let it," Alice was saying. "Mindy never really made peace with it."

I nodded appropriately, though I doubted that anyone who'd lost a loved one in the drowning would ever truly make peace with it.

"Is she seeing anyone?" I asked, cheeks burning.

Alice smiled faintly. "She was datin' someone a while back, but he was into her a lot more than she was into him."

I smiled with sympathy. "Poor guy."

She chuckled deep in her throat. "You have no idea. Anyway, I guess he eventually moved on. Haven't seen him in a while." She pursed her lips, then cocked her head. "What about you?"

I flashed a grim smile. "Not much to tell."

"Oh, I doubt that."

My finger tapped a faint cadence against the table, almost of its own accord. Try as I might, I couldn't sum up my romantic life—or lack thereof—into words that didn't paint me as anything but a pathetic weirdo. Maybe Barbara was on to something.

Alice tired of waiting and took the reins again. "You know, it always struck me as odd, you two endin' up together."

"How do you mean?"

She cradled her chin in bony hands and propped her elbows on the table. "With Carrie bein' her little sister, I mean." She leaned forward with an ambiguous smile that stretched frightfully thin. "You ever wonder why, Shane? Why you lived, I mean."

I gave Alice a wounded, sidelong glance. "You really have to ask that?"

She offered a shrug that was more apologetic than determined, yet undeniably both.

"Most days, I think of nothing else."

I sat in the car for a full minute before cranking the engine, and once on the road, I drove with no real destination in mind. I felt no desire to return to my dumpy room, yet I felt even less inclined to return to Mom's. Before I knew it, I was crossing the dam. The gulley below was divided by a serpentine trickle of water that cut between cliff-like boulders. The nose of a dune buggy peeked through the gap and then slipped back out of view.

With a nostalgic smile, I turned off by the old fire station and followed the winding road down valley terrain. Little Blue Park appeared around the bend and I took the turn without hesitation. From one end of the park, a spring-fed creek as clear and cold as glacial meltwater gurgled over flint and sandstone flats. It met the dam overflow at the foot of a waterfall, where the two merged into a swollen river.

There were several tents erected around the park, a handful of vehicles parked near the water. I pulled into a spot in the shade and strolled down to the creek. I'd forgotten how gorgeous it was here. Lush green foliage above, fish darting from rock to rock below. When you grow up surrounded by beautiful things, you can't help but take them for granted. It takes a reasonable sabbatical in more pedestrian surroundings to reset the brain. Being here now brought back a lot of good memories, but the immense beauty of the place felt brand new.

I followed the current downstream, toward the waterfall. A monster crawdad brandished its claws when I got too close to the bank, crawling into a gap between stones as I stopped to look.

Approaching the waterfall, voices resolved. I came upon a family picnicking near the creek. They smiled cheerfully but otherwise paid me no mind. A little boy—couldn't have been older than four—splashed his parents with a plastic bucket. Mom and Dad squealed in delight. Nearby, an older girl—maybe twelve—chased crawdads from rock to rock with a little minnow net trailing in the water. I couldn't help but smile in passing.

At the waterfall, a train of dune buggies was inching precariously up the boulders. They'd gain a foot, slide back two. Gain two, slide back one. It was a game of wits that sometimes took hours.

I'd learned to swim just downstream from here, where the water was a little deeper. My dad had driven me out here every day for a week, until I finally got the knack of treading water. The lakefront was closer to home, but I liked being able to see what was in the water with me.

It was good to be here again, but I probably should've quit while I was ahead. I see that now.

Just around the bend, a shirtless band of muscled-up guys was set up at the water's edge, kicked back in folding chairs around a cooler of beer. While they drank, three girls in swimsuits splashed around the shallows. They might've been friendly.

To anyone else, that is.

One of the guys glanced in my direction and abruptly sat up straight. He slapped his neighbor on the shoulder and said something rendered unintelligible by the staticky hiss of the waterfall. Soon, the entire group was gawking at me.

A guy with a shaved head rose, knocking his folding chair over, along with someone's beer. He barked something at me, and while the words themselves were unclear, the sentiment behind them was not.

I almost flipped him off—*Bring it on, asshole!*—but instead, I grinned and waved like he was my long-lost buddy. When he strutted toward me, I headed straight for him; might as well meet him halfway.

He stopped a few yards shy of me, eyes darting to the fading bruise under my eye, to the scar on my chin. The calloused knobs of my knuckles. "You need to get the hell out of here, dude," he said.

"Really? Damn, I thought you were inviting me over for a beer." I glanced up toward the brilliant sun. "Hot as hell out here. A cold one would really hit the spot."

"Seriously, man."

"Seriously," I parroted. "I'll leave when I'm good and ready."

He took a step toward me and flexed his pecs. A quick glance over his shoulder found his buddies—girls included—headed in our direction.

Sigh. "Tell you what; ask me nicely and I'll consider leaving."

The sound of his friends trudging through the flint gravel behind him seemed to embolden the guy. "Not gonna ask you again, dude. Get your sorry ass outa here before I knock your goddamn teeth out."

I had to smile at this. He was a big guy, and under different circumstances, he'd probably whip my ass. But I had a few advantages that he seemed completely oblivious to. First, I wasn't afraid to die, much less get my ass kicked. I'd been stomped half to death more times than I could count. Also, he'd been drinking, which was unlikely to work in his favor. Lastly, and perhaps most importantly?

He was barefoot.

"I would like to see that," I said, in a regrettably poor impression of Jerry Seinfeld.

With his friends now crowding around, he was committed now. And so was I. I expected him to go for a takedown—it's what

I would've done, considering the uneven terrain and lack of foot-wear—but he came at me with a flurry of punches. The first two sailed by harmlessly; the last managed to clip the edge of my chin. I saw stars for a split second, but the blow wouldn't so much as leave a mark. Another fist flew and I raised an arm, bent at the elbow, to absorb it. I didn't bother to throw a punch of my own; instead, I raised a boot and stomped as hard as I could.

Baldy went down with a shriek, his toes now splayed in all the wrong directions. The girls rushed in a panic to his aid; the boys—three of them—stepped up like they were ready to roll, but I could see the hesitation in their eyes. In their early twenties, these guys were still kids. The violence they'd grown up with was of the schoolyard variety, governed by unspoken rules, a code of honor.

I didn't have much patience for rules, much less honor.

With the whole group now present and seething over their fall-en friend, it dawned on me that they couldn't have been old enough to recognize me. Yet clearly, they did.

"You guys know who I am, or do you make a habit of starting shit with strangers at random?" I asked, though I knew the answer.

One cracked his neck like he was Dwayne Johnson and bowed his chest. He had a trite and rather sloppy barbed wire tattoo around one of his biceps. I wondered absently if he had a tramp stamp, too. "We know who you are, freak," he growled. "Everybody does."

"How?" I sincerely had to ask. "I mean, I'm way before your time." I snapped my fingers with eureka. "Wait—you guys have my picture plastered on your bedroom walls, don't you?"

"Don't flatter yourself," a blonde knockout in a pink bikini spat.

"It's okay," I quipped. "You can admit it. I know I'm hot."

Barbed Wire blew a raspberry.

One of the girls—this one on the curvy side in a black one-piece—flashed me a skittish glance. "I've seen pictures of you," she muttered. "In my dad's yearbook."

"Shut the hell up," one of the guys snapped at her. She complied, and for several long, uncomfortable seconds, the lot of them stood there without a word.

"Your friend needs a doctor," I pointed out.

All eyes shifted to the ground, where the poor bald guy had passed out. One of the girls was crying.

Dammit.

"Sorry to spoil your fun," I said. "It wasn't my intention. I guess I'll leave you to it, then."

Barbed Wire lunged forward a step and stabbed the air between us with a stiff finger. "You ain't goin' nowhere, asshole. I'm callin' the cops."

I crossed my arms, eyebrows crawling slowly up my forehead. "By all means, call 'em. They love this kind of shit—four against one, and all."

The girl in the black one piece looked uncertain.

"And I'm guessing at least one of you is drinking underage."

I gave her a wink and her eyes widened.

"But go right ahead. Give 'em a call. I'll wait." I flexed my fingers into fists at my side. "Unless you'd rather settle up like your friend?"

"C'mon, guys," Miss Pink Bikini interjected. "Let's just get out of here. Justin needs a doctor."

I waited for the verdict, fists ready to go. A few seconds ticked by and the group began a slow retreat, dragging Justin and his gimpy foot between them.

I wandered back to the car feeling like a complete dick. Why hadn't I just left? I passed the family picnic again, but they must've heard Justin's pathetic cries because when I nodded politely, they cowered back from me, like I was some kind of monster.

Maybe I was.

CHAPTER 7

July 9, 2018 ... 5:50 p.m.

I'd been preparing myself for the moment, yet when I finally crossed paths with Mindy, all that forethought mined deep into the recesses of my brain where a jack hammer couldn't have broken it free.

She didn't see me right away. A smarter man might've taken this as an opportunity to gather his wits. Me? I just gawked. Yep. Stood there like a goddamn statue with a six pack in one hand and a deli sandwich in the other.

I watched her scan groceries with trembling hands—mine, not hers—and tried to remember to breathe. When her gaze finally wandered in my direction, she froze with a bag of white rice over the scanner. Half a second passed and she looked away. The scanner beeped and I closed my eyes, letting my chin fall to my chest.

When I glanced up a moment later, a set of gray eyes skewered me. Mindy scanned the sandwich, followed by the six pack. Double bagging the beer, she didn't say a word. Not right away, that is. I'd have preferred to take her in a little at a time, but once her eyes snagged on mine, they held tight. I felt the sting of rising tears and managed to look away.

A woman wheeled her shopping cart into position behind me and began the tedious process of unloading dozens of cat food cans onto the conveyor belt.

"Heard you were in town," Mindy finally said. Her voice betrayed no anger, no bitterness. Perhaps worse, it had a faraway quality, as if spoken from across a great sea. Beyond the expanse of possibility itself.

"Yeah, I ran into the welcome committee. Guessing everyone in town knows by now." I stole another glance at her and handed over a twenty just as she nodded.

"What brings you back?"

I sighed. "My mom. She, uh…" I cleared my throat. "She passed away."

Mindy's expression sagged. "Oh, no. I'm so sorry, Shane."

"Yeah. Me, too."

Her cheeks flushed. She made change from the register drawer and handed it over with my receipt. "Will there be a service?"

"Nah, Mom didn't want anything like that."

"Oh. How long you staying, then?"

I shrugged and tried to smile. "Not sure yet."

Mindy's expression betrayed nothing.

"You look good," I said.

A faint smile tugged at her lips. "Not bad yourself, Rocky."

"You should see the other guy."

"Uh-huh."

"Still no ring," I couldn't help but point out. Mindy was by far the most beautiful woman for miles and miles. She was kind and smart, witty damn near to a fault. So what was the holdup? Not that I was complaining.

Casting a tired gaze on the old woman behind me, Mindy responded with a noncommittal shrug.

"Just waiting for the right guy to come along, huh?"

Mindy pondered a response for a moment, busying her hands with scanning cans of cat food, one at a time. "Maybe I'm not looking for a knight in shining armor," she remarked finally, just loud enough for me to hear.

"Well perfect," I quipped. "I'm not really looking for Sleeping Beauty, either. More of a Rapunzel kind of guy. Like my ladies locked away in a tower."

Mindy's head snapped back in my direction, eyes piercing, lips parting to set me straight. But her mouth clamped shut. God, she was beautiful when she was angry.

Bleep, went the scanner.

It wasn't fair, I knew, to hang the burden of my happiness on her shoulders, but I was too self-absorbed to care. I thought about Barbara's assessment; maybe I really was obsessed. It would explain a lot. Either way, I was cursed, and Mindy knew it.

From nowhere, a swell of emotion swept through me. Mindy saw it, I could tell. She saw it and knew exactly what I was thinking.

"I don't blame you," she said softly. "I didn't then, and I sure as hell don't now."

"But?"

"No buts, Shane. You went away to live your life and I stayed to live mine. That's just the way it is. Doesn't have to be anyone's fault."

I bit off a knee-jerk response to this, though my view didn't quite align with hers. I hadn't left by choice; I was driven from this town, not drawn from it. "We were good together, Mindy."

"Were we?" she snapped. "Didn't work out so well for me, last time you came around."

Last time I came around. Like I was some kind of tramp in town for a booty call. Like I could've stayed if I wanted to with her dad frothing at the mouth.

"Thirty-two fifty-four," she said to the cat lady.

"I have coupons," came a thin reply.

I left with old wounds aching like hell.

I was nineteen and a state away the second time I fell for a girl. We dated for just over a year, and somewhere along the way, I allowed myself to believe that maybe I deserved a bit of happiness after all. The way Cassidy smiled at me, the future didn't seem quite so bleak. But then, as I'd always feared it would, my past caught up to me.

I remember the way she looked at me when she finally realized who I was. That I was *that* Shane Gibson. When her image of me— forged one smile at a time over the past thirteen months—suddenly fell apart. The look on her face—utter betrayal, perhaps even horror; disgust at the very least—is something I've carried with me ever since. A humbling reminder to keep my hopes properly shackled.

Not everyone is destined for a life worth living. I was proof of that.

My room was a wasn't a sweatbox yet, but it was well on its way. I called the motel office and once again left a message. The room lacked a fridge, but hey—free AC and cable! Irritated, I ate half the deli sandwich and emptied a beer, followed by another. I was too exhausted to bother with a third, even if my fragile emotional state demanded it.

I hit the pillow and was sawing logs before I could count down from ten. The dream came on me like a wild animal, all claws and teeth. It was more vivid than usual, possibly because I now had names for the faces.

Ralph Crowley held me down as Sheriff Alan Proctor had his way with me. At the very edge of my periphery, Ray Middleton kept me compliant with constant tension on my necklace; any effort to roll away or sit up was met with a swift jerk and a few punitive moments without air. I wished Middleton would just put me out of my misery—pull that necklace tight enough to end it all. At least I'd be spared the sickening smell of Sheriff Proctor's fetid breath on my face, the revolting feel of him inside me.

Then it was over, and I could feel the man's hot seed dribble between my legs. I wanted to throw up.

When the fourth man approached to finish me off, I almost cried out with recognition. He wasn't a man at all, I realized, but a kid. Standing over me with wide, fearful eyes was none other than Jim Thompson. He couldn't have been more than sixteen, but there was no mistaking him.

"Go on, do it," Alan Proctor snapped.

The barrel trembled.

"Goddammit, son—shoot her already. We got things to do."

Jim leveled the pistol, his face screwing into a mask of conflicting emotions. The pistol fell limply to his side.

"Jesus, kid," Alan grumbled. "Hand it here, then."

The sheriff didn't hesitate. The pistol bucked in his practiced hand, blasting me square in the chest. It burned like a hot poker.

Middleton shuffled over with a mischievous grin. "Put another one in 'er. She's still breathin'."

As the sheriff pulled the hammer back to end it all, Middleton stuffed something in my mouth and let loose a guffaw at his handiwork.

My last sensation before waking was the taste of feathers.

CHAPTER 8

July 10, 2018 ... 9:30 a.m.

The next morning, Winnie and I met at Kensington Funeral Home to collect my mother's ashes. They were presented to us in a brass urn, one that might've run a hundred bucks at a reasonable establishment; we paid three fifty—plus twelve hundred for the cremation itself—inspiring Winnie to grumble all the way to the parking lot.

"Goddamn bloodsuckers! Taking advantage of folks like that, kickin' us while we're already down and—"

By the time we reached her pickup, my aunt's indignation had turned to something more vulnerable. I squeezed her arm, which was about as intimate a person could get with Winnifred without earning a stiff karate chop to the throat.

"What should we do with them?" she asked with puffy eyes,

turning the urn over in trembling hands. Her close-cropped hair was wild, her complexion paler than usual. She probably hadn't slept a wink.

"I wish I knew."

We decided to do nothing for the moment. Winnie took the urn home, dropping me off at the motel on her way. As I climbed from the truck, I paused for a moment. "Any idea where Mom's necklace came from?"

"What necklace?"

I tugged it free from my pocket. "This was in her hand."

Winnie leaned over for a closer look, then shook her head. Unless my imagination was getting the best of me though, I could swear something flickered in her eyes. It happened too quickly to interpret, but there was definitely something there. "Doesn't look familiar," she lied.

I nodded. "Yeah, okay. How about whatever was in her mouth? You saw her spit, right?"

Winnie swallowed and closed her eyes. "Jesus, I don't wanna think about that, Shane."

I expected her to leave it at that, but she didn't.

"Keep thinkin' I imagined the whole thing," she murmured, fingers strangling the steering wheel. "I think it was a feather."

Hearing my suspicion put into words, my blood turned to ice in my veins. "A feather?"

A sober nod.

I could still feel the dream bird in my mouth. "What kind?"

A noncommittal shrug. "Some kind of blackbird. Maybe a starlin'."

From the corner of my eye, I spotted the motel manager trotting in our direction. "I'll talk to you later, Winnie."

Leaning against my door with a keycard in hand, I watched her drive away.

"Mr. Gibson," the man wheezed. He was a heavy-set guy, not much older than me. I didn't recognize him, which meant that he probably hadn't grown up here. From the look of him, this was the most exercise he'd seen in a long time. Unfortunate for him, considering it was barely mid-morning, and already ninety-five degrees. Unfortunate for me too, if the AC was still kaput.

"Please, tell me it's working now," I said with hands clasped.

His face went slack. "Uh, beg your pardon?"

"The air conditioner."

His lips puckered in confusion.

"Seriously? C'mon, man. I've left you two messages. The damn thing won't come on."

"I see."

"So, can you fix it?"

"Actually, I'm gonna need you to, uh, check out, Mr. Gibson. As soon as possible."

I smiled without a trace of humor. "Is that right."

"You booked the room for two nights," he pointed out, as if that should explain the matter.

I let my gaze wander the perimeter of the parking lot; aside from my rental, there were two other vehicles. One probably belonged to this guy. "And?"

"I'm afraid I need the room. So…"

"Mister…"

"Adler."

"Mr. Adler. We both know you're hemorrhaging vacancies from your ass. So let's cut the bullshit, okay? Man up and shoot straight. What's the problem?"

The manager flushed crimson. "Mr. Gibson, I'm asking you to vacate the room. You've got an hour to clear out. Please don't make me call the cops."

I chewed my lip thoughtfully. "You know, you really ought to post a sign."

Mr. Adler frowned, wiped the sweat from his forehead. "A sign for what?"

I shrugged. "You know—one of those *right to refuse service* signs?"

The manager leaned forward, his eyes hardening by the moment. "I don't need one."

"Oh, but I think you do. And I think my buddy at the DA's office would agree." This was top-shelf bullshit, but something told me he'd be none the wiser. If he hadn't grown up here, chances were he wouldn't know the DA if she kicked him in the nuts.

"I'm not breaking any laws," he insisted, but a hint of uncertainty had crept into his voice.

"Sure you are. It's against the law to refuse me service based on my ethnicity."

Angrily, the man's hands had balled into fists. "But you're white, Mr. Gibson. And so am I."

I showed him my palms. "I'll admit, it's pretty bizarre; but clearly you're bothered by it."

"You know what? I'm calling the cops, asshole."

"Perfect!" I retorted. "You do that. Of course, there's a good chance they'll stumble across the little side business you've got going in number twelve." Gotta admit, I felt like a douchebag, using the cop card two days in a row.

Nevertheless, Adler's cheeks—rosy as Santa's only seconds ago—paled before my very eyes. "I don't know anything about that."

"Uh-huh." I decided to throw him a bone. "Tell you what, Mr. Adler. Explain to whoever's leaning on you that you've decided to keep me around for a while. So you can all keep a better eye on me. Can you do that?"

The manager opened his mouth to rebut but closed it without a word. His eyes wandered to unit twelve and back to me.

"One other thing, while we're at it," I added. "I'm gonna need two more rooms. And let's not forget that free air conditioning you've been advertising on your sign out there."

The man's eyebrows furrowed. "Two more... what the hell for?"

"That's my business. Just put it on my tab, would you? I'll swing by in a bit for the keycards."

Backing away, he stomped toward the office.

"Oh, and Mr. Adler?"

The man stopped in his tracks but didn't bother turning around.

"Let's just keep this to ourselves, shall we?"

He remained motionless for a few seconds and then stormed onward through the blistering heat.

CHAPTER 9

January 10, 1994 ... 7:15 a.m.

It was barely fifteen degrees outside; my ears burned, my nose ran. Despite the cold though, I boarded the warm school bus with trepidation. I shuffled down the aisle, praying for an empty seat. Finding one wouldn't guarantee a ride to school without incident, but it would give me half a chance. Naturally, they were all occupied. Glancing from one face to the next only managed to invite hostility.

"Hurry up, Gibson," the driver snapped. "Sit your ass down."

Swallowing hard, I tried to sit next to the smallest kid I could find.

"Go away," he barked. "This seat is saved!"

I tried the next one; a girl who had once let me play her Gameboy at recess now shot out a leg to bar the empty space next to her.

"C'mon, Gibson!"

On the verge of tears, I returned to the front of the bus. "Can you let me off, please? I think I'd rather walk."

The driver gave me an annoyed frown, but he didn't hesitate to open the door. "Do me a favor and find another way to school from now on," he grumbled as I clomped down the steps into the bitter cold.

From that day on, I got up an hour early to catch a ride with my dad. The school in nearby Ketchum was seven miles out of his way, but he didn't complain. Nor did he ask questions. By then, we both knew the score.

July 10, 2018 … 11:45 a.m.

My better sense told me it was a bad idea to come here, yet here I sat. The main entrance to the Crossroads Nursing Home campus had a cobblestone roundabout where residents were dropped off and picked up throughout the day. I was parked facing the entrance with a hand on the door handle.

Swallowing with determination, I headed inside. From behind a curved information desk, a woman welcomed me with a broad, white-dentured smile. *Gladys*, her name tag read. When I asked to see Mr. Middleton, the smile faded.

"I'm so sorry," she said with a genuinely sympathetic frown. "Mr. Middleton passed away this morning. Are you a relative?"

"No, just a, uh—" Nosy weirdo with three motel rooms? "—a

friend of the family."

"I see," she replied. "Well, I'm truly sorry for your loss."

I nodded. "Would it be possible to see his room?" I asked.

Gladys cringed. "Oh… well, I'm afraid the room has already been cleared out."

Damn.

An elderly woman inched into the main hallway from a side room, aided by a walker with tennis balls on the feet, and headed in our direction.

"I must say, it's been wonderful to see Raymond with so many visitors in his final days. I'm just sorry you missed him."

My head canted to one side. "He didn't get a lot of visitors before?"

The woman frowned. "No, I'm sorry to say he didn't."

"But he's had visitors this week."

"Oh, yes. Several gentlemen came by to see him yesterday, and another today."

"Today?"

"Yes, that's right. Probably not more than an hour before he passed."

"I don't suppose you remember any of their names? I'd like to meet up with them to pay my respects."

"I'm afraid I don't." She touched a finger to her lips and cocked her head. "Well. Except for the sheriff, of course. He came this morning."

Had Sheriff Thompson killed Middleton? If so, why?

My gaze shifted to the old woman with the walker; at her current pace, she'd reach the front desk just in time for Christmas.

"How did Raymond die?" I dared to ask.

"Well, he was very old, as you know. Any one of several conditions might've done the job. He died peacefully in his sleep, though. He didn't suffer."

"He was asleep when the sheriff came by?"

The woman's smile flickered; I was asking too many questions, I knew. Still, she answered genially enough. "Yes, I suppose he was."

"Did Ray have a phone in his room, by any chance?"

"Oh, no. The ringing tends to agitate many of our residents. We do have phones throughout the facility, though."

"I see. Are you aware of any phone calls Ray might've made this week?"

Gladys's mouth settled into a flat smile. "You know, I think I've told you all that I'm comfortable with, Mister..."

I left her standing with hands on her hips, eyes narrowed into suspicion slits. Back in the car, I read the article again and stared at the picture long and hard.

What the hell was I missing?

July 11, 2018 ... 12:04 a.m.

The welcome wagon returned just after midnight, snapping me awake with a flurry of activity outside. I sat up with an annoyed groan. On rubbery legs, I trudged to the window and peeked between the blinds. Four doors down, a mob was piled on my old room's doorstep. One of the meatheads pounded on the door again, barking something unintelligible from my vantage. When no one answered, he kicked the door in. The mob poured inside. Seconds later, seven men—each armed in some capacity—trickled back out. Confused, they stood in the parking lot and argued in hushed tones. I could almost imagine the conversation.

"What's two plus two again?"

"Quit confusin' me with that Algebra shit."

"Sorry, I just keep forgettin'. Wait—do you think Shane knows?"

"Beats me. Maybe you should ask him."

"But he ain't here."

"Huh. Good point. Hey, y'think he's got any beer in there?"

Several minutes later, they piled into three separate vehicles, which had been parked on the outer edge of the lot. Too dark to read their plates, but I smiled anyway. The lead vehicle was a Ford F150 with the words *Jack's Plumbing* plainly visible on the door.

Idiots.

When the last of the motorcade was gone, I shuffled back to bed.

Some time later, I sat up in bed with a start. I wasn't sure what disturbed my sleep this time, yet I knew instinctively that something was wrong. Fumbling in the darkness, I found my .44 on the night-stand and glanced at the alarm clock. Just after two in the morning.

I sat unmoving for thirty long seconds, listening for the slightest sound. In the distance, a cow lowed. Cars whispered by on the nearby highway. It was about as quiet as quiet got. I let the pistol fall to my lap and reached for the lamp.

That's when I saw her.

Barely visible in the shadows of one corner, she stood rigid like a waxen statue.

"Mom?" I croaked. "Is that you?"

She didn't respond.

My fingers fumbled with the lamp switch in the darkness. Heart pounding in my ears, I dared to blink; in that split second, she vanished from the corner. She was at the foot of my bed now.

"Jesus," I hissed.

The lamp finally switched on.

In the movies, light could be relied on to chase the ghosts away. But this wasn't a movie, and this sure as hell wasn't your run-of-the-mill ghost—she was nothing at all like the crotchety but otherwise harmless apparitions I'd grown up with. She took a step closer.

It wasn't my mother, incidentally. This woman was young-er, with long hair pulled back in a ponytail. She wore a dress that might've been yellow at one time but was now tattered and dis-colored by filth. Her lifeless eyes locked on me. Another step and I could see the string around her neck.

"What do you want?" I hissed, skittering to the other side of the bed.

Her mouth opened, but it wasn't sound that emerged. Rather, brackish lake water spilled down her chin and spattered her sodden dress. She shuffled to the nightstand and let her gaze fall to its surface. She picked something up and held it to her chest. My gaze shot to the bed, where my revolver remained.

Dammit. Should I make a grab for it?

As if reading my thoughts, the woman turned to look at me; I recognized the necklace dangling from her hand.

"Please," I hissed. "Just take it and go."

With milky eyes turning black as obsidian, she opened her mouth again. There was no water this time. Instead, I detected movement between her lips—something too dark and lively to be a tongue. At once, a shiny beak darted through the opening as a blackbird squeezed out and took to the air. A second emerged, practically shoved through by a third. Suddenly, birds spewed from her mouth in an angry fountain of black, flapping frantically about the room.

My lips parted in horror, too stunned to scream. I dove for the revolver and snatched up the cold metal. Leveling it at the woman, I clambered off the bed with the window at my back. Birds brushed against my skin, the deafening flap of their wings roaring like the winds of a hurricane in the confined space.

"What do you want from me?" I demanded with my finger on the trigger.

The woman dropped to her knees at the end of my bed and then fell completely from view. I rounded the bed, batting away birds as they whipped by and rustled my hair. She was gone. I bent at the waist to peek under the bed.

Nothing.

The birds whacked against the walls, scraped down the blinds. Covering my face, I made a dash for the door and yanked it open. They poured into the night, peeping and chirping frantically. When

I lowered my hands mere seconds later, the room was silent again.

For more than an hour, I lay in bed with the revolver in hand. My heart pounded, my thoughts raced. But then, from nowhere, a sense of blessed exhaustion overtook me, and I slept.

The sun hadn't been up for long when I crawled out of bed. I was tired and hungry. I showered and shaved, noting with some gratification that my shiner was almost gone.

Last night's incident was only a dream, I'd decided. One so vivid that I honestly couldn't tell the difference at the time, but a dream, nonetheless. Sometimes it takes hindsight to recognize the hallmark of an overactive imagination; looking back now, it made complete sense. The recent death of my mother, the rising intensity of my usual dreams. Combined with everything else going on, they added up to one hell of a hallucination.

I dressed quickly and headed for the door. The knob was in my hand when a passing gaze snagged on something nestled in the dingy carpet. I crouched for a closer look.

The necklace. I rose to pocket it but froze. No—not just the necklace. There was something else.

A black feather.

Glancing around the room, my pulse began to race. It wasn't a single feather, I realized. Dozens littered the floor.

"Well, shit."

CHAPTER 10

July 11, 2018 ... 8:15 a.m.

I knew it was bound to happen—especially after the incident at Little Blue—so I wasn't terribly shocked when a Mayes County cruiser pulled me over. The sheriff, like just about everyone else in town, must've heard all about the skirmish at the motel, as well as the creek. I didn't trust law enforcement, least of all Sheriff Thompson. I swiped into my phone, turned on the camera and dimmed the screen, docking the device in a hands-free clamp that hung from an air vent. Satisfied, I rolled the window down.

"Morning," the officer said genially as he reached the car, training a flashlight directly into my face. Considering the hour, the sun must've been up, but a band of storm clouds blotted the horizon, casting enough darkness to excuse a dick move like blinding a guy with a flashlight.

"Morning, Sheriff."

"Just Deputy, sir. I ain't the sheriff. Not yet, anyway."

"It's good to have aspirations," I remarked with a sickly-sweet smile, covering my eyes. I won't pretend to have been anything but relieved that this guy wasn't Sheriff Thompson, yet something about the deputy was uncomfortably familiar. And thanks to my quick wit—which truly had a mind of its own at the most inconvenient of times—I sensed an immediate shift in his demeanor.

"Uh-huh. License and registration."

I popped the glove box and shot a glance over my shoulder, squinting through the saber of that damn flashlight. "That you, Chad?"

"Deputy Mullen, to you."

"Thought so," I muttered. I handed over my registration and unbuckled to reach my wallet. Without a word, the deputy toted my documentation off to his car, where he chatted on his radio for several minutes. When the man finally returned, he wore a shit-eating grin that pretty much summed up everything I hated about this stupid town.

"Mr. Gibson, I've written up a citation for driving without your seatbelt." The deputy scrawled on a clipboard and passed it through the open window for my signature. "We take seatbelt laws very seriously in this town, sir." He smiled, showing off a mouthful of gleaming teeth.

My temper flared; I tried to tamp it down. "I had my seatbelt on."

The man leaned closer, and for a split second the predator in him shone as clear as day. "Well," he sneered. "It ain't on now, is it?"

"Listen, Chad, we both know I had it on."

"I told you, it's Deputy—"

"Let me ask you something, Chad—sorry, Deputy Skidmark—you have a dash cam in that cruiser, right? Because we both know I was buckled. I unbuckled to get my license out, and I'm betting that's on your recording. So unless you want to drag your sorry ass into court first thing Monday morning to watch footage with a judge, I suggest you cut the shit and say what you pulled me over to say."

The deputy's mouth had begun to twitch, his hands now white-knuckled on the clipboard. "I'm gonna need you to step out of your vehicle, Mr. Gibson."

Here we go, I thought, flashing a knowing glance to the camera on my phone.

Chad always was a dunce. You know the kind—every town has one. In first grade, he was the kid who ate Elmer's glue right out of the bottle. In third, he routinely farted in class and blamed it on his peers. And I'm not convinced he ever mastered the art of wiping properly.

We didn't call him Skidmark for nothing.

I'd all but forgotten until that moment, but back in high school? This idiot cheated off me in Chemistry for an entire semester. Once I wised up—and it didn't take long—I took to writing in bogus answers and correcting them after he was done copying. You'd think failing test after test would break Chad of the habit, but no. This idiot kept right on doing his thing until he flunked the class. No one ever accused Chad Mullen of being the sharpest knife in the drawer. It truly was a wonder that he'd managed to graduate at all. I'm guessing someone pulled a string or two on his behalf.

I was chuckling over this when the deputy got his hands on me. With his clipboard now on the roof of my car, he slammed me against the back door—far more vigorously than was necessary—and yanked my hands behind my back, kicking my legs apart all in one fluid motion.

"It's almost like you've done this before, Chad. You get a lot of practice out here? Harassing the tourists?"

Deputy 'Skidmark' Mullen gave the camera on his dash a nice view of his back and flipped me around. Facing me, his mouth formed a snarl. "This is for your shenanigans down at Little Blue. You broke that poor kid's toes." The weighted end of his rusty Maglite drove into my abdomen. Once, twice. Once more for good measure.

The pain was immense, but I'd endured worse. For a moment, though, I couldn't catch a breath; suffocating was a sensation that I'd come to fear above all others. The dreams had seen to that.

"Hot damn!" the deputy cackled. "That's gotta hurt like a bitch." Leaning in, he growled in my ear. "I want you to think about me when you're pissin' blood tonight. Maybe next time you'll keep your goddamn mouth shut."

He glanced over his shoulder and tipped his hat at a passing car. When its headlights disappeared around the bend, Chad leaned in again and said, "I'm gonna let you off with a warning this time."

Scumbag.

"You need to stay away from Mindy, you got it?" he was saying. "She doesn't want anything to do with you. Matter of fact, no one does in these parts. So why don't you do us all a favor and go back to whatever piss hole you call home these days?"

Glancing over my shoulder into the car, I caught a glimpse of my phone and smiled right through the pain. "Message received."

As much as Chad's handiwork hurt in the moment, it hurt a hell of a lot worse that night. As he predicted, I did indeed piss blood. The experience wasn't merely painful, it was scary. I considered a visit to the ER but quickly dismissed the idea. With my luck, some disgruntled nurse would pump me full of cyanide to avenge a lost relative.

And if I died, who would be left to complain about the air conditioner?

I attempted to take a shower and abandoned the effort as soon as the water hit me. Every movement ushered in pain; it was all I could do to climb out of the damn tub. I downed four Ibuprofen tablets and slipped into bed. Rain sighed against the walkway outside; thunder rolled in the distance. Angry and keyed up, my mind burrowed back in time, settling in to relive even more torture.

The worst day of my life.

CHAPTER 11

July 15, 1993 ... 7:10 a.m.

The visceral sounds of grief were unrelenting, but that wasn't the worst of it. A man in a black wetsuit hauled the bodies in, one by one, while officers struggled to hold parents at bay. I was close enough to make out every single face as it rolled and bobbed against the boat ramp.

Crystal Tifton.

Bobby Crenshaw.

Lindsay Watts.

Greg Flowers.

Carrie Thompson.

The bodies kept coming and coming. Their lifeless eyes gazed skyward, where a flock of turkey buzzards circled patiently. Dead blackbirds peppered the water by the hundreds. Something rustled the grass behind me; honest to God, it could've been a grizzly bear and I wouldn't have flinched. I was too despondent to care.

No one appeared to notice the woman. She had waded chest-deep into the lake, her long, wet hair framing high cheekbones and jeweled eyes. She was painfully beautiful; not in a sexual context, but an ancient one that transcended my juvenile sensibilities. Looking upon her wasn't unlike seeing the ocean for the first time; her beauty called out to me, lulled me with melodic whispers.

Without a sound, she touched each child on the forehead with a long, spindly finger. And when the last of them was beached with parents wailing nearby in horror, the woman looked in my direction and pointed an accusatory finger.

A paramedic began to disentangle me from the trotline, tugging on the treble hooks with a pair of locking forceps. It hurt, but my gaze remained fixed on the woman until she slipped beneath the surface. She didn't come back up.

The screaming didn't stop. It continued to drone in the distance even as Deputy Thompson spirited me away from the scene.

"I don't know what you did, you goddamn devil," he growled through clenched teeth, "but you're gonna pay. You can take that to the bank." His eyes were wet and pained in the rearview mirror. But more than anything, there was rage. Rage deeper than the lake itself.

July 12, 2018 … 8:15 a.m.

The annoying pulse of my cellphone prodded me awake.

"I know what to do with her ashes," Winnie blurted before I could so much as squeak out a greeting. Her voice sounded thick and congested. She'd been crying.

I sat up in bed, hissing when a stab of pain streaked down one side of my body. "I'm all ears."

"I'll pick you up in fifteen minutes. Unless you, uh…"

"It's fine, Winn. I'm alone."

"Okay. See you soon."

I dressed with considerable effort and then brushed my teeth. My eyes were puffy, my complexion paler than usual. The dreams were wearing me out.

Winnie drove us through downtown, turning off a few blocks past the library. The road meandered through hills and then dipped into a valley below the dam. There wasn't much down there, I knew. The golf course and the Grand Lake State Park. The latter was split by the river with an area for tent camping on one side and a series of RV pads on the other. Winne pulled onto the shoulder of the road just ahead of the bridge that connected the two. She killed the engine and got out with my mother's urn in the crook of one arm.

"Well, come on," she said when I didn't unbuckle fast enough.

I followed her over the guiderails into an area of woods that last night's downpour had turned into a marsh. My ribs throbbed, but I did my best to hide my discomfort. Winnie had enough on her plate without worrying about me.

We stopped thirty yards into the woods at the foot of a massive sycamore with a deadfall at its side. "This is it," she muttered.

"Um, where the hell are we?" A car whizzed by on the road far behind us.

Tears spilled down my aunt's cheeks. She plopped onto the fallen log and stroked the urn   with reverence, oblivious of the mud sucking at her boots. "Your mom took me here once, right after I moved in. It was a special place for her because…" Winnie's voice cracked, and she paused to regroup. "She was sittin' here, at this very spot, when she first realized she was pregnant with you."

My brow furrowed. "My mom took a pregnancy test in the middle of the woods?" It hardly seemed sanitary.

Winnie laughed. "No, dummy. The test came later. She just… knew, that's all."

I made no effort to veil my incredulity.

"That's the way it happens sometimes, Shane. Some women can just feel it. Anyway, she was out here one day, and out of nowhere, she just knew she was gonna have a baby. She said it was the most beautiful experience of her life, a revelation from God."

It was easy to forget how active my mom had been, back before she got sick. She'd loved to hike and explore. To draw and take pictures. She'd been fascinated by birds and insects, by the woods. With a little effort, I could imagine her sitting there in Winnie's place. A younger version of her than I'd ever seen, with black hair pulled back in a ponytail.

I swallowed back a rise of emotion and eased beside Winnie on the log.

"Your mom loved you so much, Shane."

She didn't have to tell me that, but I appreciated the gesture. "What about my dad?" I had to ask. "Did he want to have a kid?" I knew that he loved me, but who he was before his diagnosis remained an empty page in my copy of the Gibson annals.

"I don't know if he did or not, Shane, if I'm bein' honest. He was in a dark place back then, before he was diagnosed. But one thing I can tell you for sure? That man fell in love with you the moment he first held you in his arms. I was there to see the change in him." A tear streaked down her cheek. "It was like, his soul lit up with joy." She shook her head sadly, wiped her eyes. "He did the best he could to be present in those early years, but... your dad was sick."

"He never saw another woman, you know," I said. "Not the entire time I stayed with him."

She nodded. "Not surprised," she muttered. "There was only one woman for him." Her fingers caressed my mother's urn. "You know, it killed your mom to send you away."

I nodded; truth is, it killed me too. But looking back, it was the right thing to do. Whatever bitterness I might've harbored on the subject was long gone.

We were quiet for a minute, listening to a blue jay argue with a squirrel overhead. "Can I ask you something, Winnie? Something personal?"

Her eyes hardened a little, became guarded. "You can ask. Can't guarantee an answer, though."

"What happened between you and Mom? Why the RV?"

As expected, her face turned to stone. "I don't wanna talk about that, Shane. Someday, maybe. But... not now. Not today."

I nodded as if I understood, though I didn't in the least.

We scattered Mom's ashes on the ground around us, and for the first time, I allowed grief to do its thing. I cried with abandon, and at first it was for my mother. But then, the loss of my father piled on.

And finally—worst of all—thirty-six children. Their poor families.

Winnie kneaded my shoulders and cried some, too.

I was glad we came. I could feel my mom here, a sense that she truly had moved on to a better place. That everything was going to be okay.

My aunt invited me over for breakfast, but I demurred. I wanted to be alone for a little while. I should probably get packed and ready to hit the road.

CHAPTER 12

July 12, 2018 ... 10:45 a.m.

My suitcase remained in the corner, ignored. My mother was at rest now, so what was still I doing there? I honestly couldn't say if it was pride or something more substantial. I had a life back in St. Louis—a comfortable apartment and a decent job. A 401k. I drove a forklift for a manufacturing plant. Far from glamorous, but it paid the bills. No one gave me shit there, not the guys I sparred with after hours, not even my frat-boy neighbors. I didn't have a girlfriend, but I did have a few female friends with benefits. It wasn't much, but it was a life.

So what in God's name was keeping me here?

There was a timid knock on my door. I gasped on my way out of bed. A sickly bruise the size of a grapefruit contrasted like ink against my pale skin. I reached for a shirt and yelped.

The knock came again, this time a little more insistent.

I gave up on the shirt and opened the door a crack.

"Hey," Mindy said.

"Hey." I opened the door a little wider. "How'd you find me?"

She gave me a wry grin. Backlit by the late-morning sun, her skin glowing in golden hues, Mindy was nothing short of breathtaking. "The grapevine never sleeps around here," she chuffed. "You oughta know that better than anyone."

"The room, I mean."

Her grin skewed into a sheepish slant, her eyes darting to my boots on the walkway. I must've rinsed five pounds of mud from them before putting them outside to dry.

I chuckled deep in my throat.

"So, can I come in?"

I took a step back and she brushed past me. Inside, her gaze bounced from the tired carpet to a framed painting over the bed—a meadow peppered by obscure shapes that might've been recognizable as deer, if not for a grimy layer of nicotine-stained filth—and then the bed itself, whose castoff sheets betrayed a mattress that dipped in the middle like a bowl. Finally, her attention settled on the twenty-year-old television at the end of the bed.

"Wow," she snickered. "Is that thing even color?"

"Free AC and cable, too." A smirk was on my lips, but the sight of a feather at Mindy's feet sent it packing. I'd tried to get rid of them all, but they kept popping up. Maybe it was time to switch rooms again.

Mindy chuffed, and for a second I couldn't remember what was funny.

Oh, yeah. Free AC. "Seriously. That's what it says on the sign."

"Does it really?" Mindy peered between the miniblinds for a view of the sign. "Are there motels that don't have AC and cable? Might as well throw doors on there, too. *Free AC and cable, plus a door that opens and closes.*"

"Has a nice ring to it."

Mindy shrugged. Hair spun from pure, sun-dappled honey slipped off her shoulder and settled against the swell of her tank top. I tried not to notice. I tried very hard not to remember the feel of her skin against mine, the taste of her lips. The—

"We all have our gifts," she said through a throaty laugh. "Too bad mine isn't..." Her words trailed off at the sight of my bruised torso. "Oh, my God," she muttered. She took a step toward me, leaning over for a closer look. "Have you seen a doctor for that?"

"Sure," I lied.

Mindy reached a hand out to touch it, hesitating at the last millisecond. "Does it hurt?"

"Nah."

Her head swiveled up to admonish me. "Liar."

Delicate fingers brushed my skin, drawing goosebumps up my arms. She prodded the area gently. "Does it hurt when I touch it?"

It didn't, and I was about to say so when a bolt of lightning racked my whole body. "Jesus," I hissed.

"Don't tell me *that* didn't hurt, Shane. You need to see a doctor."

"I'm fine," I insisted.

"You have a broken rib. Maybe more than one."

"And you would know this... how?"

Mindy gave me a mildly wounded look. "I went to nursing school, asshole."

My eyebrows shot up. "You did? When?"

"Few years back."

"Oh, my God, Mindy," I remarked. "That's great!"

I was about to ask what happened—why a woman with a nursing degree was sacking groceries, that is—when the answer dawned on me. Nurses probably had access to pills. I wondered how long it took for Mindy to succumb to the temptation, or if her reputation had simply preceded her.

Without a word, she looked away. "Is there a point in asking who did this?"

"I fell in the shower."

Her gaze whipped back to me, eyebrows bunched with annoyance. "Uh-huh."

With a half-smile, I took another stab. "Wait, I ran into a door."

She folded her arms across her chest with an impassive gaze.

"Um, I got kicked by a horse?"

Rolling her eyes, Mindy couldn't quite hide her smile. "You are such a smartass. Does it hurt to breathe at all?"

"A little," I admitted. "But it's bearable."

"Coughing up any blood?"

"Nope." No sense mentioning the blood showing up in other places.

"Well if that happens, you'd better get to the hospital. Could mean a punctured lung."

"Yes, Nurse Ratched."

She shook her head with a sad smile. "You really should go

home, Shane."

I thought about my apartment, the testosterone machines I called neighbors—who routinely got drunk and peed off the balcony, by the way. "What if I don't wanna go home?"

Mindy's face grew serious. "Why are you still here?"

As always, a snide remark was on my tongue, but I bit it back for once. "Kind of wondering the same thing. I guess I have unfinished business."

"With who?"

I looked away.

"You're gonna get yourself killed."

I glanced back to her, flashing a crooked smile. "Maybe. Probably. But I'll die a little happier, seeing you first."

She rose with stormy eyes. That's the way it was with her. Fire and ice. "Don't do that, Shane. Don't make me part of your death wish."

The corners of my mouth turned down. "I've already tried running, you know. It isn't all it's cracked up to be."

"Go home, Shane. Be happy."

How could she possibly understand? I wasn't capable of being happy. Not in St. Louis, not here. Not on a beach with a cocktail in my hand. Not without her.

"Come with me." The words slipped the leash even before I knew they were coming. But they were heartfelt, so I made no effort to take them back.

Mindy's gaze turned to glass and slid to the floor. She plopped onto the edge of the bed. "I can't."

"You can't, or you won't?"

"Is there a difference?"

Not really. "Of course there is."

"It isn't fair, Shane. What you're doing."

I cocked my head and let that speak for itself.

Her nostrils flared. "I've got enough shit to deal with already, you know."

I did. At least, I thought I did. Nevertheless, a life on the move with my gypsy of a dad had taught me the art of selfishness, and I wasn't above wielding it now. "Did you love me, Mindy?"

Her eyes squeezed shut. "Stop it. Please."

On some level, I wanted to, but I couldn't help myself. "C'mon. It's a simple question."

Mindy sniffled. "That was a long time ago."

"Was it?" She was right, of course. We were just kids. Still, a broken heart can't be reasoned with; despite no small effort, mine remained frozen in time, indifferent to the days piling up like dead leaves. I eased onto the bed next to her. "Why'd you come here, Mindy? To convince me to leave?"

She didn't reply.

"Look me in the eye and tell me you don't still think about me."

With lips stretched thin, Mindy shot to her feet. "Coming here was a mistake," she muttered. "I gotta go."

Before I could sputter a word of protest, she darted to the door and wrenched it open, slamming it shut in her wake. The impact shook the whole wall, rattling the nearby window in its aluminum frame and sending the miniblinds into a slow sway.

I grunted to my feet and padded barefoot to the door, leaning my forehead against it in defeat. Tears were gathering, and I didn't bother holding them back. My outing with Winnie still fresh on my mind, I was a hot mess; at this point, it would take more out of me to repress the pain than to let it burn.

Maybe Mindy was right. Every minute here was a strain on my emotional state. Maybe I *should* go home. Water my plant, get rid of last week's takeout leftovers. Spar with Adam. Have a beer with the neighbors and get back to my routine.

Without thinking, I opened the door to watch Mindy walk to her car—because I was a glutton for torture, apparently—only, she wasn't in the parking lot. Rather, she lingered mere feet away, statuesque on the walkway.

"Are you okay?" I asked, wiping my face dry.

Suddenly, her lips were on mine, her arms snaking around me frantically. My side burned in protest, but the pain faded to a whisper. Then we were in the bed, and with each kiss, each frenzied touch, the world seemed to fall further out of focus.

The anger and grief, the soul-eating survivor's guilt—the overwhelming misery of being me—it all fell away to reveal the great emptiness within. And for a short while, the only person who could possibly fill the void made me whole again.

CHAPTER 13

July 12, 2018 … 12:10 p.m.

The anniversary was mere days away now, and the whole town seemed to be holding its breath. The tension brought out the worst in the townsfolk. Neighbors squabbled over stray cats, drivers honked and flipped the bird over the tiniest infraction. I should've known better than to venture out, but Mindy was at work and I was bored. And starving.

What happened next shouldn't have caught me by surprise, yet it did. I stopped by a Mexican restaurant for lunch; I wasn't a big fan of dining alone, but I'd grown used to it over the years.

The owner—a compact boulder of a man—met me at the door, barring me from entry.

"Sorry, we're closed," he said. His eyes were cold and unabashed.

My cheeks flushed. "Sure about that? Parking lot's pretty full."

A flat smile. "I'm sure."

I could've thrown a fit, of course. But if I had learned anything in my short time back, it was to choose my battles. And a burrito wasn't a hill worth dying on.

Pissed, but no less hungry, I drove farther into town. The high schoolers working at Sonic didn't know or give a shit who I was. I tipped my carhop five bucks and watched her face widen with delight.

I ate my burger and tater tots in a stew, watching absently as cars buzzed by. I thought about calling Adam, back in St. Louis. Fresh out of law school, he had a hard on for social injustices. He'd wipe that Mexican restaurant off the map in a heartbeat.

There was a sharp rap on the passenger-side window. "That you, Shane?" a bearded man asked, his face cupped against the window.

There was no stifling my grin at the sight of him. "Mike Owen?"

My old friend laughed merrily.

I rolled down the window. "Oh, my God! How the hell are you?"

"Doin' good, brother. It's been way too long."

It sure had. "Hop in and cool off, man. It's hot out there."

Mike waved this off. "I better not. Got the kiddos with me." He stabbed a thumb over his shoulder toward a red SUV. Indeed, three mini humans craned in their seats for a look out the window.

"Someone had sex with you?" I jibed. "More than once?"

"I know, right?" Mike laughed merrily, a sound that was wonderfully familiar yet weathered by time. "You in town for long?"

"Not sure yet. A few more days, I guess."

Mike's smile faded. "I heard about your mom. Real sorry for your loss, man. She was a good woman."

"Thanks, Mike. Means a lot."

He glanced back to his vehicle, then to me again. "Listen, why don't you come over for dinner tonight? Tabitha would love to see you."

My heart warmed at the thought, though Tabitha Burrows had never spoken a word to me, back in school. "Tabitha married you? Dear Lord, what has the world come to?"

His eyebrows bounced provocatively. "What can I say? I'm a hot piece of meat."

I let loose a guffaw.

"Seriously, Shane. You should come."

I considered the offer. "Can I bring a guest?"

Mike grinned. "Absolutely."

I left Mindy a third voicemail. Why was she dodging my calls? I knew she was working, but surely she got a break. Was it really too much to ask for a quick text? It was tempting to drop in on her, but I resisted; the line between checking on her wellbeing and stalking the woman felt frightfully thin. Still, I needed to get out of my room. The dinginess of the place was beginning to wear me down.

I was getting into my rental when a long-haired guy jogged over from room twelve. "Something I can help you with?" I asked warily, stepping away from my car.

"All good, man. Your girlfriend—she was asking about some Oxy. Just wanted to let y'all know I got a line on some. It'll be tomorrow, though."

My gut tightened. "When?"

"I don't know. Probably ten or eleven." He gave me a *What can you do?* sort of shrug. "It'll be here when it gets here."

"No, I mean when did you talk to her?"

The kid nodded, shoved his hands in his pockets. "This morning. On her way out."

"She buy anything?"

His eyes narrowed suspiciously, but he kept his cool. "Just a little crystal."

I nodded and leaned in. "What's your name, man?"

"Kenny."

"Okay. Do me a solid, Kenny. If my girlfriend approaches you again, I want you to send her away. Can you do that?"

Kenny's expression hardened. "Like hell."

I gave him a patient smile that probably dripped with condescension, but hey—I did try. "I know, it's a lot to ask. But I'd really appreciate it. She's trying hard to stay clean, you know?"

A defiant smirk. "It's a free country."

With a sigh, I leaned a little closer. "Is it?"

The kid had a couple of inches on me, but that was about the only thing he had going for him. Even the knife he whipped out worked against him. It was too long and flashy; I saw it coming and put him on the concrete even before the blade cleared the sheath in his waistband.

From the ground, he took an angry swipe at thin air.

"Don't be an asshole, Kenny," I grumbled.

He reared back for another swipe and I kicked the knife from his hand; it twirled across the parking lot and landed with a clatter.

"You need to quit while you're ahead, kid. You're starting to piss me off."

"You're dead, mother—"

"Whoa," I admonished him. "Let's watch the language, Kenny. This is a family establishment. Free AC and cable, and all that."

He tried and failed to kick me in the knee; I snatched his foot as it arced past and locked it in the crook of my elbow, pivoting on the balls of my feet to put pressure on the joint.

Kenny howled.

"Don't piss me off any more than you already have," I snapped. "Now, are you ready to be civil?"

He nodded profusely.

"Good." I released his foot and let him clamber to his feet.

He struggled to keep his balance, favoring his left foot. Wincing with chest heaving mightily, Kenny stabbed the air with an angry finger. "You're messing with the wrong people," he seethed.

My arms folded across my chest. "I'm not messing with anyone, Kenny. I asked you for a small favor, and you just had to be a dick about it."

He stormed back toward his room, hobbling and growling under his breath.

"Hey, kid," I barked after him.

He hesitated with his hand on the door latch, glaring over his shoulder.

"Don't do anything stupid. You got a good thing going here.

It'd be a shame to burn your bridges over a few pills."

Defiantly, he powered through the door and slammed it behind him.

"Good talk," I muttered and returned to my car.

I called Mindy and hung up when she didn't answer.

Mike Owen lived on a five-acre plot just outside of town. His home was a modest but well-built bungalow, surrounded by towering trees. I couldn't have masked my envy if my life depended on it.

Tabitha gave me a hug that had me gasping. "Sorry! Did I hurt you?"

I laughed it off, though I was practically seeing stars. "Not at all," I grunted. "That was a yelp of pleasure."

She snickered. "God. How are you and Mike not related?"

Next, I met the kids. Jayden—the oldest—was twelve, followed by ten-year-old Ruth and finally Hunter, whose third birthday was only a few weeks away.

Mike offered me a beer and we ventured onto the back deck to chat.

"So, where's your date?" he wanted to know.

"Yeah, sorry. Fell through at the last minute." I glanced at my phone irritably. No missed calls, no text messages. Nothing.

"Her loss, buddy."

Smiling sadly, I allowed myself to pretend that Mike didn't know exactly whose loss it really was.

We clinked bottles and sat back in the shade to enjoy the scenery.

The rear of Mike's property sloped downhill, which made for a particularly beautiful view of untouched forest. I sipped my beer and watched Jayden and Ruth chase grasshoppers by the tree line.

"This is amazing, man. Beautiful family, beautiful home. I'd be lying if I said I wasn't jealous as hell."

"I'm blessed, no doubt about it." Mike took a swig from his bottle and shook his head. "Damn, it's good to see you, man." The glow of his smile dimmed a notch. "Prob'ly hard to come back, huh?"

I shrugged. "There are places I'd rather be, not gonna lie."

He nodded. "You stayin' at the house?"

Down the hill a bit, Ruth caught a grasshopper and bounced with excitement. "Look, Jayden! I got a big one!" Her smile could only be described as incandescent; she reminded me of Carrie.

"Nah," I sighed. "Got a room at the Starboard Inn."

His eyes crossed. "Yuk, dude."

"It's not that bad." I flashed a sheepish smile. "Free AC and cable."

"Well, if you get tired of roaches nibblin' on your toes, the couch here is always free."

"Thanks, bud. I'll keep that in mind."

As we fell silent, a menagerie of childhood memories whispered for my attention; for once, I let myself give in.

Catching crawdads with Mike and Riley.

Watching tourists climb the Grand River Valley in souped-up Jeeps and dune buggies.

Cannon balls off the bluffs by Scotty's Cove.

Sneaking our first taste of beer.

We'd been best friends since we could walk, Mike and me. Despite the rumors surrounding me, he'd stuck by me. But then there was the drowning, and everything changed. Mike's parents, like most, took charge of his social life. At least, where it pertained to me. Sure, he'd still wave at me in passing, even slap me an occasional high five when the adults weren't looking, but it would never be the same between us. At best, we'd be reduced to hallway acquaintances.

"The anniversary's comin' up," he said quietly. A second passed and he chuckled. "Guess I don't need to tell you that, do I?"

I took a deep breath. "Nope."

"You gonna be okay?"

I nodded. "Yeah, man. I just wish there was something I could do, you know?"

Mike finished off his beer with a belch. "There's a pretty big group of volunteers plannin' to guard the shoreline."

"That's great." I wouldn't be welcome on that committee, of course, but it was nice to know the townsfolk had something more proactive in mind than burning me at the stake. "You volunteering?"

His gaze shifted toward the woods, coming to rest on Ruth. "Bet your ass, I am."

"You gonna lock her in, too?"

"Tabitha's takin' the kids to stay with her parents in Grove."

"Even better."

Mike chewed his lip, shaking his head at an unwelcome memory. "You know, I'll never forget that day. The way those screams carried across the lake." His eyes had turned pink at the corners. "I'm so grateful you didn't die, Shane."

I felt the wistfulness of the evening turn bitter. "You know, after the incident," I replied evenly, "people told me all the time how lucky I was to survive."

Mike nodded, blinking back tears.

I finished my beer and tried to smile. "I believed them. For a while."

My old friend wiped his eyes. "I can't even imagine how hard it's been for you, man. I remember school was pretty rough—" Possibly the understatement of the year. "—but I really hoped things would get better for you after you moved."

"They did."

The back door creaked open and Tabitha leaned out. "Dinner's ready!" she hollered down the hill.

From inside, little Hunter barreled through the doorway and plowed into his daddy's lap. Mike snatched him up with a merry cackle, beaming like the sun itself. My chest hitched at the sight. Had I ever been that happy before? I didn't think so. Honestly, I couldn't even imagine what that kind of happy felt like.

We ate pork chops and corn on the cob, followed by ice-cold watermelon. With bellies full, we retired to the deck again to watch the kids chase fireflies.

I remembered nights like this, before the drowning. Carefree and innocent, without a fear in the world. I remembered, but it took effort. The drowning claimed more than thirty-six lives; it overpowered all but my strongest childhood memories.

Sometimes I wondered if it erased the better part of me, and if the shitty leftovers deserved to remain at all. But then moments like these came along to give me hope.

CHAPTER 14

July 12, 2018 ... 5:35 p.m.

I was waiting in the Reasor's parking lot when Mindy got off work the next day. She gave me a shy wave and then stopped abruptly, her smile gone in an instant.

Chad Mullen seemed to appear from thin air, squeezing between cars in a determined stride toward Mindy. For a moment, I was too stunned to react. He said something indecipherable to Mindy and gestured over his shoulder. I took a peek behind me and caught a glimpse of his patrol car, two rows back. Jesus. How long had he been there?

I stepped from my car and headed in their direction. Mindy's eyes flicked to me and then back to the deputy. "Chad, we've already talked about this," she was saying. "I'm just not interested in you like that, okay?"

"Everything alright, guys?" I asked.

Mindy flashed a worried smile. "We're fine. Deputy Mullen was just saying hello."

I stopped a few feet away. Chad turned to size me up. Slowly, a corner of his mouth rose. "Not real good with following instructions, are you? Was I not clear?"

"Crystal. Only, I figured it was more of a suggestion." I turned to Mindy and nodded toward my car. "You hungry?"

"I could eat."

Chad's smirk turned into a sneer. "She ain't going nowhere with you." When Mindy made a move to leave, he snatched her arm and held her stationary.

My blood boiled. God, I wanted to beat his ass to the moon and back. Fortunately, better sense prevailed. I took a small step in his direction. "You see that up there, Chad?" I pointed up the nearest light pole, where the black dome of a security camera budded near the top.

He stole a quick glance, squinting slightly. "So?"

"So, at this very moment, your assault on this young lady is being recorded. Her manager is also watching."

Chad turned to glare at the store manager, who stood in the cart atrium with a phone glued to his ear. The deputy's grip loosened, and Mindy tore free.

"You've got a real knack for screwing up on camera, Deputy," I pointed out helpfully. "One of these days, it's gonna bite you in the ass."

Chad looked ready to put a bullet in my head. He bowed his chest and closed the distance between us. "Might as well be today.

Don't think for a second a few cameras are gonna save you."

I inched closer to him. "Oh, I don't need saving."

"Stop it, you two," Mindy snapped.

I sighed. "Someday, Skidmark. But not today."

"You think you can talk to me like that and just walk away?" he balked.

"Yep," I quipped. "I do. But before we take off, there's something you should probably see." Slowly and deliberately—for the benefit of the camera, as well as any witnesses—I showed my empty hands. "I'm gonna take my phone from my pocket now, okay? I'm unarmed."

Chad's eyes darted to Mindy and then to the store entrance, where a few bystanders had congregated to watch.

I swiped my phone awake and opened my YouTube app. I picked a video and scrubbed forward on the timeline a bit. I hit play, facing the phone toward the deputy just as the screen came to life.

There were three distinct thumps as he worked me over with the flashlight, followed by Chad's muffled but unmistakable voice.

"God damn! That's gotta hurt like a bitch."

I watched the deputy's face pale as he recognized his ugly likeness, perfectly framed by the car window.

"I want you to think about me when you're pissin' blood tonight. Maybe next time you'll keep your goddamn mouth shut."

His eyes had widened with uncertainty. "Turn it off," he snapped.

Under the circumstances, I didn't feel obligated to follow any orders. "Just a sec," I chuckled. "We're getting to my favorite part."

"You need to stay away from Mindy, you got it? She doesn't want

anything to do with you. Matter of fact, no one does in these parts. So why don't you—"

He'd seen enough. Angrily, the deputy snatched my phone and reared back to smash it against the ground. At the last millisecond, he remembered that he was being watched. Leaning in, he slapped the phone against my chest. I caught it before it could fall and swiped into my camera.

He stabbed an angry finger at me. "You'd better delete that or—"

I aimed the camera at him. "Or what? Are you threatening to assault me again?"

From nowhere, another officer appeared at Chad's side, this one dressed in police blues. He waved to the store manager and then turned to appraise the lot of us.

I let the phone fall to my side. "David Griffin?" I exclaimed with a genuine grin. "Holy smokes! Long time no see, brother."

His face lit up. "Well, look what the cat dragged in! How the hell are ya, Shane?" He slapped me on the shoulder, and I winced as the impact rippled across my ribcage. "Heard you were in town. Was hoping to run into you sooner or later."

"Well, I'd call this your lucky day, then."

He chuckled. "You should swing by the gym while you're in town. Do a little sparring?"

"Yeah, sure."

The officer split a wide grin. "Looks like you could use a little practice, man. Just sayin'."

"Ah, the shiner. That's the last time I go after some kid's milk money."

We both snickered and David grew serious. "So what's the story here?" He peered around, gaze bouncing from face to face. We'd managed to attract a pretty respectable audience for such a small town.

"Oh, nothing," I lied. "Mindy and I were just leaving."

David turned to Mindy. "That right?"

Her eyes darted to Chad and back. "Yeah."

The officer gave a slight nod, turning his attention to Chad. "Something I can help you with, Deputy?"

Chad crossed his arms. "Nope."

"Well, good. Good. You have yourself a good night, then."

The two lawmen glared at each other, neither willing to give an inch. Mindy and I didn't stick around for the pissing match. We had better things to do.

Back in the car, Mindy took my hand and gave it a squeeze. "I'm so sorry about that, Shane. I went out to dinner with Chad one time. It was my dad's idea, and it was a complete disaster."

"Don't worry about it. You can't take credit for him being an asshole. That's definitely a preexisting condition."

She leaned her head against my shoulder with a pouting grin. "Thanks for not judging me."

"Have you talked to your dad about Chad? Seems like he'd put a stop to that bullshit."

Mindy grimaced. "Maybe. But it might just escalate things."

I nodded, though I wasn't entirely convinced.

"Listen, Shane. I'm really sorry about yesterday; I must've turned off my ringer."

Her words teased a memory from the darkest corner of my

thoughts. *Just a little crystal*, Kenny had said. Had Mindy already smoked or snorted it—or whatever the hell people did with meth?

I tried to smile and managed something that might've resembled one. One of Winnie's favorite maxims seemed to whisper in my ear.

Anyone who lies about the little things will damn sure lie about the big things.

CHAPTER 15

July 10, 2018 ... 8:15 a.m.

From the parking lot, Barry's Gym hadn't changed a bit since I left at sixteen. Same faded sign, windows still plastered with old newspapers. David was on the heavy bag when I let myself in. There were a few unfamiliar faces, but otherwise we had the place to ourselves.

David Griffin was on a very short list of friends from my adolescence. He moved to the area when he was fifteen, long after the drowning. While my other peers were contemptuous, David was kind. And unlike me, he wasn't afraid to stand up for himself. If not for his tutelage, I'd have cowered in the face of confrontation well into adulthood.

"So what's the story with the shiner?" he wanted to know

I flashed an enigmatic smile. "C'mon, man. You know the first rule of fight club."

My old friend smirked. "You serious?"

"Nah. Just a fender bender."

He unloaded a lightning-fast combination, sending the bag into a violent sway. "Explains that shitty rental you've been driving around. What the hell is that thing, anyway?"

I shrugged. "I'm thinking a Sebring, but it's hard to say with no decals. Has the pep of a dying sloth."

David shook his head in disapproval. "Whose fault was it?"

"Oh, a little old lady. Ran a red light and t-boned me."

"Damn, that sucks." He threw another combination, bobbing and weaving as the bag pendulummed to and fro. "What kind of car was it?"

"Hers? A Lincoln Town Car."

"Yours, dumbass."

My grin faded. "'65 Mustang, candy-apple red. My dad and I restored it together before he died. Wasn't a scratch on it before the wreck."

It was one of the last things we'd done together as father and son, incidentally. The cancer had consumed him faster than I'd imagined possible. Whereas my mother would later wither away over the course of a year, my dad departed this world less than a month after his diagnosis.

David let his gloves drop and nodded sympathetically. "Damn, that's a shame."

I put on a smile and did my best to shrug the memories off. We dug up an extra pair of gloves and moved to the ring for a few rounds.

"Watch the body shots, if you don't mind," I remarked. "I'm a little sore."

We both took it easy, but even still, I caught a stiff blow to the ribs and damn near passed out. David snatched my shirt and took a look underneath.

"Jesus, Shane. A little sore, my ass! Anything broken?"

"Probably."

"Why the hell didn't you say something?"

He was right, of course; it was a dumb move. I'd allowed my need to feel something familiar to outweigh my common sense. And not for the first time, if I'm being honest. I was no different than Mindy in that regard; my insatiability took a different form than hers, but we both knew the pull of that invisible leash. The feeling of helplessness, the ever-present gravity of shame.

David leaned forward for a better look and clicked his tongue. "You know, that shiner's practically healed, but this… it looks pretty fresh. Skidmark's doing, by any chance?"

"Very astute, my friend. You should be a detective."

David scowled. "God, that guy's an asshole. Without that badge, he's nothing but a bag of stupid."

I nodded. "He's slimy, no doubt about it. With any other sheriff in office, he'd be locked up instead of deputized."

David's easy-going demeanor stretched taut. "Watch your ass with these guys, man. Sheriff Thompson's a real piece of work."

"Yeah, that's what I hear."

David yanked off his gloves and began to unravel the tape around his knuckles. "I'm serious," he said. "All summer long, he's been strutting around like a damn peacock, just daring anyone to cross him."

"Oh, yeah? Why's that?"

"He spearheaded a drug bust back in May. Didn't get any dealers off the street, but he confiscated twenty kilos of meth. Pretty significant haul for such a small town. Made a big splash at the time, but now the buzz is starting to fade. Wouldn't surprise me in the least if he went after you just to make a show of things. Campaign season's right around the corner, you know."

"Isn't there an age cap?"

David shrugged. "If so, maybe he just wants to go out with a bang."

"Yeah, well. I guess he knows where to find me."

Winnie called to invite me out to dinner. I agreed, though I'd have preferred a quiet evening in with Mindy. I hadn't been able to reach her all day. Again. It was her day off; we hadn't made any specific plans, but I'd assumed we'd spend it together. I should've known better than to assume anything where Mindy was concerned.

Winnie insisted on driving, which proved to be a pretty scary experience. She slipped off the asphalt onto the grass shoulder too many times to count, for one. And it didn't help that she drove twenty miles over the speed limit. I had to close my eyes as we crossed the narrow Pensacola dam to keep from pissing myself.

Cosby's was packed with a ten-minute wait. But as anyone who's ever eaten there will undoubtedly confirm, the food is well worth the wait. Winnie and I stood by the door patiently, sustained by the mouthwatering aroma of fried cuisine. The weight of a hundred eyes hung on me every damn minute. While a few patrons glared openly, most stole surreptitious glances, looking away if I happened to catch their eye. Yet as awkward as the wait was, a glance over Winnie's shoulder after we were seated offered assurance that the evening was about to get a whole lot worse.

Sheriff Thompson glared daggers through me. And across from him—with his back to Winnie—was good old Skidmark Mullen. He turned in his seat to give me a smug grin.

Fan-frickin-tastic.

Our server brought sweet tea and took our orders. Winnie went with the all-you-can-eat catfish. I'd intended to do the same, but my stomach shrank to half its size under the sheriff's withering gaze. I settled for fried chicken and sent the waitress on her way.

Patrons came and went, but for more than an hour, the sheriff and his dipshit deputy held tight to their table. Likewise, Winnie refused to leave until she got her money's worth of catfish. Didn't matter that I was picking up the check; there were principles at stake.

Ralph Crowley showed up at one point, and I just about lost it. Fortunately, the old man didn't stay long. When his gaze landed on the sheriff, he didn't amble over to say hello. On the contrary, Crowley's face wrinkled with distaste as if he'd just smelled a particularly robust fart. He left discreetly.

I'd known that Sheriff Thompson would come at me sooner or later. It turned out to be sooner. Winnie and I were halfway to the pickup when the man stormed over, scattering gravel in his zeal. "Just what the hell are you doin' here, Gibson?"

"I'm visiting family and friends, Sheriff. That okay with you?"

"Hell no, it ain't okay. Emotions are runnin' hot enough as it is. Don't hardly need you stirrin' shit up even worse."

"Is that what I'm doing?"

"Damn right, y'are."

"And what exactly am I doing to 'stir shit up'?"

Sheriff Thompson took a step closer, leaning in until I could smell the catfish on his breath. I saw him through the old woman's eyes for a moment, just a scared adolescent grappling with uncertainty. "You're breathin' in public, ain't ya?" he glowered.

"With respect to breathing in public, Sheriff: I'm pretty sure you're the one people should be worried about." I let my nose wrinkle in disgust. "Good Lord, you could really use a Tic Tac. Maybe a good handful."

His cheeks flushed, his eyes gleamed. He opened his mouth to snarl a retort, yet—to my surprise—something seemed to flicker behind his eyes like a shadow shifting positions, and he changed his mind. Shaking off his irritation, the sheriff's expression softened. "Real sorry about your mom," he muttered.

Oddly, I could tell he meant it. It was perhaps the kindest thing Jim Thompson had ever said to me. I was about to file it away with the most bizarre of my life experiences when he spoke again.

"You have my sympathy, both of you. Truly." Some heat returned to his eyes. "That said, you need to get the hell out of town, Shane. You hear me?"

Thus far, Winnie had managed to keep her cool; the mention of her sister, though—however sincere the sentiment—seemed to light her fuse. Squeezing between the sheriff and me, she stuck a thick finger in his face.

"This ain't your town, Jim. But you just keep on overstepping your bounds, by all means. See if I don't sue your ass into the dirt again."

The sheriff's eyes never left mine. "No problem," he said with a flat smile. "I've said my piece." His boots pivoted in the gravel as he strutted back to his Chevy Tahoe, white with blue law enforcement signage. From within the vehicle, Chad looked on with a lizard smile—leaving his mark on the passenger seat, no doubt. Sheriff Thompson had a foot on the running board when he stopped and turned back to me.

"One more thing, Gibson!" he bellowed across the lot. "Stay the hell away from my daughter!"

With rage damming up within, I showed him a fist and cranked an invisible reel with my other hand; my middle finger rose like a crane, slowly and deliberately.

I know, I know—I was pushing my luck. Thing is, I just couldn't help myself.

Winnie elbowed me in the side, drawing a grunt of pain.

"Dammit, what the hell, Winn?" I gasped with a hand on my ribs.

"Don't go poking the bear, Shane." She was right, of course.

Once we were buckled in, I turned an inquisitive gaze on my aunt. "So what's this about a lawsuit?"

My aunt gave me a sidelong glance. "You didn't know? Your parents and me, we filed a civil suit against him back in '93."

My eyes bugged. "Holy shit. What for?"

"Unlawful detainment of a minor. Harassment. Something

along those lines."

"And you won?"

Her plump cheeks bunched into a wide grin. "Damn right, we did."

A belt sander couldn't have wiped the joy off my face.

August 26, 1995 ... 10:25 p.m.

I was twelve the first time we kissed. I was sprawled on a dock at Yonker's Marina. The place had gone out of business by then. Officially, it was the recession. But everyone knew better. The stigma of the drowning had pulled the marina under. Few came around here anymore. I suppose if every town has its haunted house on the hill, this had become ours.

I was staring up at the stars when she appeared from nowhere. One second I was alone, tracking a satellite amidst the stars; the next, she was looking down on me. The faraway banter of her friends carried across the cove.

"Hey," Mindy said.

I sat up to look at her. "Hey."

"Whusha you lookin' at?"

Her words were slurred, but I was too young to put two and two together. I could only shrug, unsure of what to say.

She plopped to the deck and leaned against me. Her friends burst out laughing at something, then went quiet again. Cigarette embers flared in the darkness like fireflies.

"Thought I was the only one who came here anymore," she said.

I gave her a shrug and wondered how many others came here for solitude, thinking the same thing. Mothers and fathers, revisiting the innocent cove that had claimed their beloved children. All those bodies, their placid faces—

"I miss Carrie," Mindy whispered, drawing me from the maw of that ravenous memory.

"Yeah. Me, too."

We sat in silence for a while, the dock creaking and swaying in the darkness. Water gurgled pleasantly against the empty boat slips. It was kind of nice.

I was supposed to be fishing, but my dad must've known better when he dropped me off. I'd come to ponder this place, desperate to make peace with it. Later, my dad would pick me up without a word. He'd just squeeze my shoulder and nod. He was like that—a man who spoke volumes without saying a word. He'd skip town mere weeks later, once my mom filed for divorce.

A light breeze blew Mindy's bangs aside, unveiling wet cheeks in the moonlight. She was so beautiful.

"I'm glad you're still alive," she said.

I swallowed bitterly. "That makes one of us."

"What's that s'pposa mean?"

I opened my mouth to reply, but the enormity of my self-loathing was too much to put into words. Her hands found my face in the darkness and pulled me in. She tasted of peach wine coolers and cigarettes. When we parted, she giggled.

"What was that for?" I had to ask, nearly breathless.

She ran her fingers through my hair and down the back of my neck. "I don't know. Incentive to keep livin', I guess."

From across the lagoon, a lone voice called out. "You comin', or what?"

Mindy cupped a hand around her mouth and yelled, "Be there in second!" Turning back to me, she sighed. "Don't tell anyone, 'kay?"

And just like that, she was gone.

CHAPTER 16

July 11, 2018 … 7:45 a.m.

Mindy called me early the next morning. I picked up with relief and a twinge of indignation.

"Hey, you," she said with a smile in her voice.

"Hey, back. What happened yesterday?"

She hesitated. "Oh, shit. I guess I forgot to tell you. I was helping my mom remove some wallpaper yesterday. We're fixing up her sewing room."

If it was a lie, it rolled off her tongue like honey. "Sounds fun."

"Oh, my God—you have no idea. You up for breakfast?"

My stomach growled in assent, but the rest of me was still on guard. "Maybe. I'm supposed to help Winnie wash the neighborhood strays."

"Smartass," she giggled.

"Seriously, though. Seems like everywhere I go, someone gets all worked up."

Mindy sighed. "Well then, you'll just have to come here for breakfast."

A smile bewitched my lips. "You're gonna cook for me?"

Mindy blew a raspberry. "Me? Afraid not. You'll be doing the cooking."

"What about your roommate?"

"She's been staying at her boyfriend's the last few days."

Grinning, I rubbed the sleep from my eyes. "Well, then. Your wish is my command, my queen."

"Mm, I like the sound of that."

Half an hour later, I rapped on the door of her small apartment. "It's open!" she yelled from within. I found her in the kitchen, beating half a dozen eggs with a plastic whisk.

"I thought I was doing the cooking."

She dropped the whisk, batting eyes the color of stormy seas. "I do *not* have a problem with that," she said with a laugh. "But you'll need this." She untied her apron and sauntered forward to drape it over my shoulder.

At once, my eyes popped out of my skull and bounced across the room. My unmentionables tore a hole through my jeans and impaled a cabinet door.

Well, that's what it felt like, anyway.

Mindy leaned in for a kiss on my neck, pulling me close. "Cat got your tongue, Shane? You act like you've never seen me naked before."

I don't recall much about the food, but... wow. Best breakfast ever.

Later, we curled up on the living room couch. Mindy flipped channels on television, but I was far more interested in watching her. To say that she was beautiful would be a colossal understatement. I wondered how she managed to get through the day without stopping traffic. Without men falling at her feet in worship.

"What are you looking at?" she giggled.

"You."

"Well, quit." She slapped me playfully on the thigh. "You're making me feel self-conscious."

"Sorry, no can do."

Mindy turned to me with pursed lips, eyes drooping seductively. "I have ways of making you obey."

"Oh, is that right?"

"Don't test me."

Laughing, I held up my hands. "Please don't call your dad."

Abruptly, Mindy's smile went limp.

"Shit," I muttered. "I'm sorry, that wasn't funny."

She looked away. "There's something wrong with that man, Shane. And he still has it in for you."

"Preaching to the choir, my dear."

Her eyes slipped closed. "It's my fault."

I felt what remained of my smile fall apart. "Like hell it is. He's hated me as long as I can remember."

"You're not the only one he hates, just so you know. I've been on his shit list even longer than you."

"Your dad cares about you, Mindy."

The sea of her gaze darkened, threatening to swallow me whole.

"What would you know about it?"

"I know he goes out of his way to protect you from me. Even though he's wrong about me, it says something that he bothers."

"That ain't love, Shane. That's just marking territory. It's what he does."

Rolling my lips, I nodded. Maybe she was right—what would I know? "I'm sorry. That was presumptuous of me."

"Yes, it was."

I leaned across the couch and dragged her into my arms. "How can I make it up to you?"

She giggled half-heartedly, then fell silent. Her eyes drifted over my shoulder and lost focus. "The anniversary's almost here."

"Yeah, I know."

She pulled away gently and clasped her hands over one knee. "A bunch of us are supposed to guard the shoreline."

"I heard about that. Sounds like a great idea." I swallowed hard and looked away. "You think it'll happen again?"

Mindy shrugged. "I don't know. But this town won't survive if it does."

She was right about that.

Squeezing my hand, Mindy sighed. "I think about Carrie every day. Constantly, sometimes. She was the good daughter, you know."

I ran my fingers through a lock of her hair. "Don't sell yourself short, Mindy."

She shook her head slightly. "I'm not just saying that, Shane. My little sister was more pure-hearted than anyone I've ever known." Her eyes were wet now, brimming with tears. "It should've been me. I was the screw-up."

I pulled her into an embrace. "Please, don't say that, Mindy. It isn't true."

"It's what my daddy says," she mumbled into my shoulder.

I felt my loathing for the man turn into something much more substantial. "Yeah, well your dad's a heartless dick, and that's about the best I can say about him."

We were both quiet for a while. Mindy was the first to break the silence.

"You realize what's gonna happen if anyone drowns?"

"I can guess."

She pushed free of my embrace to look me in the eye. "I'm scared, Shane. For the kids of this town. For you."

I ran a finger down her cheek. "You know, there is an easy solution to all this."

Her eyes squeezed shut. "I can't go with you, Shane."

"Why not? What's keeping you here?"

She didn't speak for a moment, tracing the veins on the back of my hand with a manicured fingertip. "I have a life here," she finally said. "It may not be much, but it's mine."

Funny—I often thought of my existence back in St. Louis in those precise terms. Only in my case, it was a grudging acceptance of my crappy fate rather than an excuse to settle for less than true happiness.

Likewise, her voice had a wounded quality that belied something familiar—something else I could relate to. I took a stab in the dark. "You don't think you deserve a better life, do you?" I muttered. "This is your penance."

She shrugged but didn't deny it.

"C'mon, Mindy. Punishing yourself won't change a thing. There's a big world out there. We can explore it together."

Her shoulders sagged. "I can't, Shane. It just… it wouldn't be right."

"Are you kidding? You have as much a right to happiness as—"

Her eyes turned to ice, her nostrils flared. "No, I don't. You don't understand, Shane. It was my fault, Carrie dying."

I swear, my heart sprung a leak for her in that moment. "Jesus, Mindy. Please tell me you don't really believe that."

"It's true. If I'd been there with her, she'd never have gotten outside."

This admission gave me pause. As far as I knew, she'd been asleep in bed when Carrie let herself out. It's what she'd always told me. "What exactly are you saying?"

"I snuck out that night, after everyone was asleep. I…" Her head fell and a fat tear slapped her thigh. "I left her all alone, Shane."

"Where'd you go?"

She buried her face in her hands. "Please don't ask me that."

A terrible disquiet rose within me, squeezing my guts like a fist. "What did you do, Mindy?"

"Shane, please. It doesn't matter." She looked up with burdened eyes. "The point is, I wasn't there to protect Carrie."

I wanted to trust her—no, I *did* trust her—but this secret of hers, however small or irrelevant, felt like a mountain rising between us. "What could you possibly have done? You were, what—twelve? Thirteen?"

Mindy was silent.

"If you did something, Mindy, please don't let me find out from someone else."

She buried her face in her hands again, shaking her head.

The temptation to bulldog the truth out of her was almost more than I could handle. I hated that she was keeping me in the dark. About that night. About the drugs, and who knew what else. Yet as much as I wanted answers, I was terrified by what might be revealed. What if beneath all the white lies was something unforgiveable? Something that would ruin everything?

With a sigh, I scratched her back. "Okay," I relented. "I'll leave it alone."

For now, anyway.

CHAPTER 17

July 12, 2018 … 5:25 a.m.

It was just shy of the butt crack of dawn when Mike rapped on my window. I opened the door in a weird, half-sleeping daze. I hadn't slept well; rather, I'd untangled my last conversation with Mindy and tried to weave it back together again, over and over, like tying and untying knots. I really didn't want to answer the door. But I was a man of my word. At least, I thought I was. Hard to nail something like that down when you're only half conscious.

"Ready?" Mike asked with way too much enthusiasm for such an ungodly hour.

"I guess."

"C'mon, brother. Give it a chance. You're gonna love it."

"Says every guy just before he takes a girl's virginity."

"My, my," Mike snickered. "Such cynical wit at this early hour."

Ugh. I'd never gotten the whole fishing thing. Don't get me wrong—I didn't begrudge those who did, and there was always a chance that I'd change my mind someday—but I gotta be honest: the waking before dawn bullshit alone was a pretty blatant strike one.

We headed out in Mike's pickup. Our first order of business was at The Dam Stop for coffee and donuts.

"Remember when we'd crack up over the name of this place?" I cackled through a yawn.

Slurping from his coffee, Mike grinned. "Wait—you don't still do that?"

There was a lot to like about Mike. He was kind and honest—altruistic to a fault. But my favorite thing about the guy had always been his smile. You could almost ignore what the rest of his face was doing; he lit up in the eyes like no one I'd ever known. It was damn near impossible to maintain a proper pouting with him around—believe me, I'd tried too many times to count.

Back when Sheriff Thompson was just a deputy, he convinced me that Mike had implicated me in the deaths of those kids. Almost as much as the drowning itself, falling for that cruel ruse had ruined me. Until that day, I'd honestly believed that grownups were universally bound to the truth, that only bank robbers and Nazis could be driven to such vile manipulation. That I'd been gullible enough to believe Jim Thompson remains one of my strongest regrets. I've never forgiven myself for it.

And the worst part?

Selling me the lie had gained the deputy jack shit; there'd simply been nothing to confess in that interrogation room.

We catfished off the bank for an hour, kicked back in folding chairs with our coffee. The sun was on the rise—a beautiful sight, there at the water's edge. I took it in with awe. A little too much awe, as it turned out. My pole—wedged upright between a tree root and a slab of river rock—bent over and then toppled to the ground.

"Woo hoo!" Mike howled. "Get 'em, man!"

I grabbed the pole and gave it a quick jerk to set the hook. I kept tension on the line as I reeled, just as I'd been taught as a kid. It didn't feel like a fish on there. Not that I'd caught many, so my frame of reference probably wasn't very reliable. It took five minutes to get it to shore.

"Ah, damn," Mike muttered. "I was afraid of that. It's a slider."

"A what?"

Before he could respond, the crest of a turtle shell broke the surface a few feet out.

"Oh, man."

Mike was unsheathing a knife from his belt. "Drag it over this way, wouldja?"

The knife gleamed in the morning light and I hesitated. "Listen, I didn't sign up for a beheading."

"He's got your hook, man."

"So what? I've got more. He's worth more than a hook."

Mike's eyes softened. "Listen, Shane. I know it seems cruel, killin' this thing. But lettin' it go would be even more cruel."

"How's that?"

"He swallowed your hook, man. It'll shred his insides if we let him go. It might take hours or even days, but one way or the other, he's gonna die. Believe me, a quick death is the best thing for this guy."

Strike two.

Twenty minutes later, while I was still pouting, I got a decent fish on the line. To my dismay, I lost it when my line hung up on something and snapped. Mike faired similarly, but—as always—his spirits never wavered.

When it was all said and done, Mike ended up with two catfish—neither big enough to keep—and a two-pound bass. As for me, I managed to get a drum all the way in.

We were halfway home when it hit me for the first time—the appeal of fishing, that is. Sure, getting a fish on the line was exciting, but that wasn't my takeaway from the morning. It was the shedding of my burdens, however temporary the reprieve. The peace. Throughout those two hours, I hadn't wasted more than a cursory thought on the craziness that was my life. If not for that poor turtle, it might've been the most relaxing morning I'd known in a very long time.

"You up for second breakfast? Tabitha's prob'ly scramblin' some eggs about now."

My stomach rumbled a plea, but I demurred. "Maybe some other time, bud. I'm pretty tuckered out."

He wanted to say something—I could see it in his eyes—but he merely nodded and turned his gaze back to the road. "Thanks for comin' with me, Shane. I feel like I've been given a second chance to be a better friend."

"Right back at ya, brother."

"Next time we'll take the boat out. Fishin's a whole lot easier when you can go where the fish are."

"Sounds good. But I gotta ask—is fishing after, say, ten o'clock a thing?"

Mike laughed. "Sure, if you're lookin' for a good scorchin'."

It was a little after eight when Mike dropped me off at the Starboard Inn. My coffee had worn off by then, yet the depth of my exhaustion was more than could be explained by kicking back in a chair for the morning. Funny how quickly the stress settled back in after a morning off. The sting of being in this town, the perpetual resurgence of memories best left forgotten. The weight of it all nagged incessantly. Despite my intentions—however vague they were at the moment—I knew I couldn't maintain this for long. The fallout from this visit was taking a heavier toll than I'd realized.

I stripped, piling my clothes in the bathroom. They were smattered with worm guts and fish slime. I debated the merits of burning them as opposed to washing them; at an impasse, I left them to ferment on the tile floor. I should shower, I knew.

But...

I crawled into bed and closed my eyes. The dream came quicker than ever.

There truly was no rest for the likes of me.

A truck with the words *Jack's Plumbing* on the doors was parked at the library later that morning. My hackles rose instinctively, but I fought them back down.

Jean looked up from her computer. "You're still in town?" she exclaimed.

"Yep." My lips curled at the smell of urine. "Got a leak or something?"

She frowned. "Ugh. One of the toilets is backed up in the men's restroom."

"Nice."

Her eyes flicked off to one side where a dark-skinned girl in her mid-twenties was unpacking a box of books. She wore a badge emblazoned with the word VOLUNTEER rather than an identifying name. Jean lowered her voice. "You realize what tomorrow is, don't you?"

A flash of irritation surged through me; I closed my eyes and fought it down. "Better than most."

She nodded and began to chew her lip.

Biting back my angst, I tried on a plastic smile. "Can I borrow that magnificent brain of yours again?"

"Ah, Shane. Flattery will get you everywhere, old friend."

I relaxed a little. "Thank God."

"And donuts, incidentally."

I smiled—the real thing this time. "Flattery will get me donuts? I'll keep that in mind for next time. I'm partial to apple fritters, just so you know."

"Ah, the smartassery is strong with this one," she laughed. "So what kind of scavenger hunt are we on today?"

My smile weakened. "A woman was murdered somewhere around here, back before we were born."

Jean chewed on her lip some more. "Hmm. Well, that's not much to go on. Can you be any more specific?"

"She was old. And Indian—not sure what tribe."

Jean gave me a knowing stare, and if I didn't know better, I'd swear she was trying to read my mind. With a shrug, she sighed in what might've been defeat. "Better than nothing, I guess. Let's see what we can find."

An old man approached the desk with a pile of paperbacks. His eyes darted to me and back to the desk. Turning to her volunteer, Jean said, "Rhea, are you comfortable manning the desk for a while?"

The younger woman gave her a thumbs up and returned to the tedium of applying call number stickers to the spines of a mountain of books. The old man cleared his throat. Rhea rose to her knees to peek over the desk, offering an apologetic smile. "I'm sorry, sir. Didn't see you there. Ready to check out?"

"Yes, ma'am. What's with the smell in here today?"

Jean and I made a dash for the stairwell.

Back into the basement we went, pillaging the library's collection of newspapers. With no specific date range to work with, it felt an awful lot like finding a needle in a haystack. But at least it didn't reek like a latrine down there.

"How old do you think Sheriff Thompson is?" I wanted to know.

Jean stiffened. "Why? You think he has something to do with the death you mentioned?"

"I don't know. Maybe."

Jean's lips stretched into thin slivers of pink. "I hope you're being careful, Shane. Maybe you should just ask Mindy."

I gave her a deadpan stare.

"What, like you two are supposed to be a secret in this town? Might as well shout it from the rooftops. Hell, I would."

I rewarded this with a snicker that quickly faded, then a sober nod. "I'd rather not bother her about it. Her dad's kind of a sore spot."

Jean tapped her chin with a fingertip for several seconds. At once, her eyes widened. "Aha!" she exclaimed. Without another word, she dashed back upstairs. I followed with a little less zeal, still exhausted from my early rising, and in no particular rush to be re-acquainted with the smell of piss upstairs. At the front desk, Jean's fingers flurried over a keyboard, interrupted every few seconds by a mouse click.

"Got it!" she said with triumph. She swiveled her monitor for me to see.

"What am I looking at?" I muttered, leaning forward.

"Thompson is an elected official."

"Okay…"

"So, elected officials don't enjoy the same anonymity as the rest of us." She pointed to a date on the screen.

April 11, 1952.

"That's his birthdate," she explained.

I made a mental tally. Sheriff Thompson would've been sixteen in 1968; of course, I couldn't be sure of his age in the dream. "That narrows it down quite a bit," I said. "Let's try from 1965 to 1970."

Back downstairs we went. As it turned out, I should've trusted my gut. We found what we were looking for in one of the 1968 issues of the Tribune. On July 15th of that year, an elderly Cherokee woman was found dead on the side of a country road. She'd been beaten, raped and shot dead. She carried no purse or wallet, much less a driver's license, and therefore could not be identified.

We sifted through the next ten issues for a follow-up story before throwing in the towel. Not a single mention of the woman, not even an obituary. Frustrated, we headed back upstairs.

"You'd think it would be big news, right?" Jean remarked thoughtfully, plopping into her chair at the circulation desk. "I mean, a brutal murder in a town this size? Seems like the whole community would've been in an uproar."

"It was a different world back then," I pointed out. "Not a good time or place to be Indian."

Jean frowned. "That's true. But still…" She shook her head. "I gotta say, this feels all wrong to me."

"Oh, I couldn't agree more."

From nowhere, a thought struck like lightning. I yanked the necklace from my pocket. "I've been meaning to get your opinion on this. What do you make of it?"

Jean dug a pair of bifocals from her desk drawer and examined the artifact. "These beads look like bone," she observed. "It seems old. Where'd you find it?"

"Long story. The beads have symbols on them. Any idea what they mean?"

Rhea shuffled over, making no effort to veil her eavesdropping. Jean inspected each bead reverently but shook her head in the end.

"Okay, then. Any idea who might shed some light on it?"

Rhea cleared her throat. When I turned to look at her, her dark skin had paled. "Um, I think I've seen those before," she said in a mousy voice.

Jean and I gave her our full attention. "Seriously?" Jean asked, her mouth slightly agape.

A timid nod. "Almost positive. I mean, I don't know anything about them, but… I think I know who you should talk to."

The *Jack's Plumbing* truck was gone when I left, but the owner had left me a thoughtful parting gift. On the hood of my rental car, a glop of chewing tobacco glistened in the sun, as did a shiny scratch that spanned the length of the passenger side.

Have I mentioned how much I hated this town?

Carl Whitehorse lived in a small mobile home outside of Bernice. Per Rhea's instructions, I zeroed my odometer on my way out of Langley and slowed when it reached seventeen miles. Glancing from the mileage display to the road, I spotted the man waving from a break in the tree line ahead. With a hooked thumb, he directed me down a weeded path that might've been a gravel drive, once upon a time.

Carl must've been in his eighties, but he carried himself with the vigor of a much younger man. His hair was long and gray with wisps of stubborn black peppered throughout.

With a paper bag pinned in the crook of my arm, I climbed from the rental car and shook his hand. "Shane," I said in introduction, careful to omit my last name.

"I know who you are," he replied solemnly. "My great granddaughter filled me in."

My eyebrows shot up. "And you're still willing to talk to me?"

He frowned deeply. "The townies fear what they don't understand. And they seem to understand a little less every day."

I nodded. "Well, thank you."

"Don't thank me yet. I might turn out to be a waste of your time."

Inside, he offered me a drink. "Actually," I said, "I brought a little something for you. Rhea tells me you're a bourbon man." I opened the paper bag to reveal a bottle of Jack Daniels. "I'd have gone for something fancier if I knew a damn thing about bourbon."

The old man's mouth stretched into a wide grin, flaunting shiny gums without a tooth in sight. He cracked the bottle open and took a swig. "Oh, that's good stuff. You want some?"

"No thanks. I'm driving."

He nodded and gestured toward a couch. We both sat.

"So, did you bring it with you?"

"I did." From my pocket, I produced the necklace.

Carl accepted it and ran calloused fingers over the beads. "This is definitely old," he informed me.

I'd surmised as much.

"Mind if I ask where you got it?" he wanted to know.

"My mother."

His eyes flicked over to me. "She gave it to you?"

"Not exactly."

He shrugged, then examined the artifact more closely. "By God, I think this was hers," he whispered in awe.

I assumed he was referring to my mother; accordingly, I remained silent.

Carl rose from the couch and wandered down the hallway into the trailer's only bedroom. I could hear him shuffling around back there, though I didn't have the slightest idea what he was looking for. I appraised the living room in his absence. It was decorated with the usual Native American tributes—a painting depicting the Trail of Tears, another of a warrior chief with an eagle-feathered headpiece, a shadow box containing arrowheads, that sort of thing—as well as a smattering of Coca-Cola memorabilia. There were pictures too, but Carl reappeared before I got around to them.

His eyes were downtrodden.

"Everything okay?"

He nodded sadly and plopped to the couch next to me. In one hand, he held the necklace; in the other, an old photograph. "She was my aunt," he explained, handing the photo over gingerly.

It was old and overexposed, depicting a woman in traditional Cherokee attire. Indeed, she wore a necklace that resembled the one I'd brought with me.

"Name was Awinita Kitua," Carl told me.

I nodded politely, but I wasn't convinced. Sure, Langley was a small town—and nearby Bernice was even smaller—but honestly, what were the odds? Besides, the photo was far from definitive proof. The image was degraded, devoid of the fine details needed to identify the necklace with any certainty.

Carl took another gulp from the whiskey bottle, smacking his lips. "She was murdered," he added. "Raped and shot dead back in the sixties."

I felt the blood drain from my face. Okay, so the odds were better than I thought.

"They never caught the killer," he remarked, taking another nip from the bottle. "Not like they looked real hard, though. The law didn't give a damn. We were less than second-class citizens, back then." He grunted with a sour frown. "Still feels like it sometimes, if you ask me."

So there it was. After decades, I finally had a name for the woman in my dreams. Part of me was desperate to quit while I was ahead, to hunker down alone and process it all. But the rest of me couldn't tear my eyes from Carl. This man knew things, and however ridiculous my story was likely to sound, something about the old Indian told me he'd at least keep a straight face if I confided in him. And if my gut was to be believed, the man might have more insight to offer. Still, getting those first words out wasn't as easy as it sounds.

The last time I'd confessed my dreams aloud, I was seventeen. My father had put me in counseling the very next day. My therapist was nice enough, but she threw me back on meds and spent the next several months trying to dissect my psyche, determined to unpack some kind of Freudian symbolism from my dreams—symbolism that simply didn't exist.

Was I really prepared to open that can of worms again?

Like it or not, I realized, the can was already open. I needed help from an unbiased third party—one who wasn't paid by the hour to psychoanalyze me. One who understood the esoteric significance of who I was.

"I've been dreaming about this woman," I told him. "Awinita, I mean."

Carl went rigid. "Dreams should never be ignored."

"Even the ones where you're running around in your underwear, trying to figure out where your clothes are?"

The old man didn't crack a smile. "Tell me," he said.

I hesitated. "They're pretty unpleasant, Carl."

He folded his arms and waited me out. So I told him, leaving nothing out. His eyes were leaking when I finished, and I was a little surprised to find my own wet.

"I'm sorry, Carl," I sighed. "For your loss, and for the pain I brought to your doorstep today."

He put on a stoic smile. "That's very kind of you, Shane. But I'm truly grateful to finally know what happened. The truth gets ugly, but that don't make it any less important."

I clasped my hands and took a moment to appraise the old man. I've known a lot of people his age—enough to realize that years don't necessarily add up to wisdom. Carl Whitehorse was an exceptional man.

"Let me ask you sumthin, Shane. Have you ever thought about why you survived?"

Okay, scratch that assessment. Despite myself, I wanted to slap him upside the head.

I must've bristled visibly, because Carl held up a hand of apology. "Course you have," he chuckled. "Stupid question. What about now, though? Knowing what you know."

I blinked. "Are you suggesting the drowning had something to do with your aunt?"

"Maybe. Not just my aunt, though."

This time, I waited *him* out.

"Awinita and her sister—my mother—were forced off their land back in '43 when the townies diverted the Grand River to fill the lake. Land my family called home for many generations."

"Did they own it on paper?"

Carl nodded. "Didn't matter, though. Eminent domain. They flooded it without so much as a letter of warning. I remember wakin' one morning to find six inches of water at the foot of our porch steps. The whole house was under water by the end of the week."

"Holy shit..." I muttered.

"They call that area of the lake Drownin' Creek. I'll tell you, it really lived up to the name that day."

I nodded, but then caught myself. "Wait, you're saying it was called that *before* 1993?"

"Oh, yes. Some folks say we came up with the name b'cause the creek had a tendency to dry up out of the blue. It was spring fed, y'see—it ran independent of the water table—so it was confoundin', the way it came and went. But that had nuthin' to do with the name."

I leaned forward, stupefied. I'd never bothered to question the misnomer—that Drowning Creek wasn't a creek at all, but a leg of Grand Lake; likewise, I'd never questioned the origin of its name because I thought I already knew.

"Truth is, that area—the very spot where all those children died?—it's a cursed place. Even 'fore the drownin' of '68, it was a place to be feared. I grew up hearin' stories of animals drownin' themselves in that creek. Deer, birds. Horses. Not just animals, neither." He paused to bow his head. "My aunt had two children. Her little girl died on that stretch of water, even 'fore there was a lake."

"Oh, my God..."

Carl nodded somberly. "Weirdest thing. Awinita found my little cousin floatin' in the creek one mornin'. She was a good swimmer too, and the water wasn't that deep. Nobody really knows what happened."

My stomach squirmed. "Jesus. What about her other child?"

"Oh, he was drafted and sent off to Vietnam. He didn't make it back home."

"That poor woman."

Carl reached for the bottle, then changed his mind.

"Carl, earlier, you made a reference to the drowning of 1968. You meant '93, right?"

A sage smile. "No, sir."

"So what happened in 1968—it was another drowning?"

"Guessin' you never heard about that, huh?"

I could only shake my head. As far as I knew, the incident was the best kept secret in the county.

"Not surprised. Most folks wouldn't know the details. And the few who do know better than to talk about it."

I swallowed hard. "Will you tell *me* about it?"

Carl sucked on his lower lip contemplatively, and for a while I expected him to backpedal. But eventually, he nodded. "Best to keep this to yourself, though, hear?"

I nodded.

"So, once upon a time, twelve fellas headed down Drownin' Creek to fish. They left early in the mornin' and never made it back. A search team went lookin' for 'em the next day." He snatched up the bottle and took a nip. "We found 'em all dead. Every damn one." Another pull off the bottle, this one longer. "I'm guessin' you can figure out when and where."

I managed a breathless nod. "You were there?"

He closed his eyes and rolled his lips. "One of the volunteers.

We found their canoes tied to trees near the shore—there wasn't a marina there back then, not even a proper boat ramp. The bodies were just… floatin' nearby. Not a scratch on 'em."

"Holy shit…"

The old man grunted in agreement. "Tourism was already strugglin'. The sheriff and the powers that be, they didn't want nuthin to do with it. Never even opened an investigation."

"Why not?"

Carl leaned forward, and for the first time, a flash of rage rose from the depths of his features. "'Cause it was just a bunch of goddamn Injuns, that's why!"

I stiffened under his wrath.

The old man looked away, jowls flushed and trembling with emotion. "They were good people. I grew up with 'em. Seeing 'em like that…" He took a wavering breath and released it through the hollows of his dentures. "Some things, you just wish you could unsee."

"I can't believe this is the first time I'm hearing about this."

Carl shrugged, now deflated of his anger. "Only a few of us knew the details, and we weren't exactly inclined to talk about it. The sheriff saw to that."

"He threatened you?"

"Told the whole search party we'd end up like our buddies if we breathed a word." He paused to scratch his chin. "Awinita was found dead later that same day, you know. The newspaper caught wind of it, but someone shut them up, too."

"Jesus," I muttered.

"Ain't many alive who know the truth no more."

My frown deepened. "Everyone knows something happened. That year—1968—it's even more infamous than 9/11 around here."

"Funny how that works, ain't it?"

I nodded, though it wasn't funny at all. My hands had balled into fists. Yet beneath the anger, things made a little more sense, now. Why this particular year was so significant—why everyone was so damned convinced another drowning was imminent. The tragedy of '93 hadn't been an isolated incident at all; it was a datapoint in a measurable trend.

I swallowed to clear the nerves from my throat. "Carl, there's something I haven't told you. Haven't told anyone, actually."

He nodded and wiped his eyes, now cloudy from the whiskey.

"I, um… well, I saw a woman in the water when I was a kid. Right after the drowning."

The old man crossed his arms. "Ain't surprised."

"Uh, you're not?"

"You didn't survive by accident, Shane."

Thinking back, remembering those fishhooks in my leg, I wasn't so sure. "The woman pointed at me, Carl. Right at me. Like… I don't know—an accusation. She was angry."

Carl sighed. "Ain't sure what to make of that, Shane. But if she'd wanted you dead, you'd be dead. I can promise you that." He scratched his chin. "Maybe she was pointin' at someone else. Way I heard it, folks practically swarmed Yonker's that mornin'."

I wish I had half his confidence. "Who exactly are we talking about, anyway? Awinita?"

Carl's eyebrows jumped. "Oh, no. I'm talkin' 'bout the Lady of the Water."

I was no expert in Native American folklore, but I'd never heard of anything even remotely like what he was describing. My expression must've told all.

"Don't believe me, do ya?" he chuckled.

"Please don't take it personally. I'm not sure what to believe anymore."

"Every body of water has one, you know. The woman you saw, she's always been there, in Drownin' Creek. Even 'fore the lake came along."

"But why the mass drowning? Thirty-six kids—an entire generation. The scale is beyond comprehension."

"Maybe she wanted vengeance."

"For who?"

"All of us, I s'pose. For floodin' the land fifty years earlier. The death and displacement of indigenous people. For Awinita. Your guess is as good as mine."

It was becoming harder by the moment to accept any of this tangent at face value, but I kept my skepticism to myself. It was me who'd opened this can of worms, after all.

"She'll prob'ly appear again, you realize."

I nodded, suddenly deflated. "Tomorrow's the drowning anniversary."

"Yes, I s'pose it is, ain'it? More will die, I s'pect."

My heart ached at the thought. "More children?"

Carl's chin dropped sadly to his chest. "Hard to say."

"What can we do to stop it?"

"Nuthin, Shane. Curses like this have no end."

My eyes stung with frustration. "But if she wants vengeance, why doesn't she just go after the people who deserve it?"

Carl took one of my hands in his own; it was a brazen gesture that should've felt awkward yet didn't. "Wish I knew the answer to that question, Shane. God help me, I really do. But who's to say who deserves to live or die?"

I offered the necklace to Carl—it was a family heirloom, after all—but he declined. "Sumthin tells me you might need it for a while. After things blow over, maybe then."

I returned to my motel lost in thought, fondling the beads with tingling fingers. My mother—how had she gotten her hands on the necklace? She was connected somehow. For now, how would just have to remain a mystery.

CHAPTER 18

July 12, 2018 ... 8:15 p.m.

The six of us filled the biggest booth Mo's Café had to offer. David and his wife Callie sat across from Mike and Tabitha, leaving Mindy sandwiched against the window across from me.

Barbara was off for the night, thank God; I didn't have the energy to endure her disapproving presence tonight.

"Jean's not coming?" David wanted to know.

I shook my head with a frown. "Nah, something came up."

Mike sighed with exaggerated relief, which—as much as I loved Mike—rubbed me the wrong way.

"She's a good person, Mike," I said with some heat. "That's all that should matter."

Mindy kicked me under the table, punctuated by a smoldering glare.

Callie snickered. As for Mike, he almost managed to keep a straight face. "You don't have to tell me that, man," he said with a laugh ringing at the edge of his voice.

My eyebrows hiked uncertainly up my forehead. "Uh, I don't?"

"He doesn't know, Mike," David chimed in with a snicker. "How could he?"

I blanched and dared to ask, "Know what?"

Eyes twinkling, God bless him, Mike put me out of my misery. "Jean's engaged to my older sister," he explained.

"Oh," I replied with cheeks burning. "I see."

Mike finally reached around Tabitha to slap me on the back. "Don't sweat it, man. It don't bother me in the least. Thing is though, they can get a little loud."

Tabitha blew a raspberry. "Oh, my God. That's putting it mildly. 'Specially once they've had a drink or two."

"Well, aren't we a progressive bunch?" I chuckled. I grinned, allowing my gaze to bounce around the table. Funny how I'd managed to convince myself the whole town abhorred me; here I was, surrounded by proof that humanity wasn't all bad.

We ordered burgers and fries—a side salad for Callie, who was watching her figure—and settled in to catch up. It warmed my heart to see Mindy smiling, laughing with abandon at Mike's corny jokes, swapping amused whispers with the other ladies. I'd never seen her so at ease.

With our bellies full, Mike suggested a nightcap at The Dam Tavern. "They've got karaoke," he added with eyebrows bouncing.

It was tempting—the thought of Mike belting out some Lynyrd Skynyrd with a few beers in him was truly amusing—but I decided to quit while I was ahead. "I've got a feeling that showing up at a bar tonight would be pushing my luck."

I stole a glance at David, who nodded sagely. "Probably true."

Mike wasn't ready to let it go. "Okay, so how about our place?"

"Um, I don't think so, sweetie," Tabitha interjected, her tone singsong with warning.

"Why not? We can have the sitter stick around a little while longer."

"I don't want to wake the kids."

Mike sighed and lowered his voice. "We'll be quiet, hun. I promise."

His wife crossed her arms knowingly. "You always say that."

"Yeah, but I really mean it this time."

Mindy giggled.

"Some other time, Mike," David promised. "We've gotta be up bright and early, anyway."

Mike relented with a frown. "Bunch of party poopers."

"Alyssa's boyfriend is staying over tonight," Mindy told me on her way into the car. "Maybe we can go to your place?"

"Sure thing."

Her hand tickled my thigh as we pulled from the lot. It glided higher and came to rest on my zipper.

"Whoa," I laughed. "Uh, what are you doing?"

"You just keep your eye on the road," she said in a breathy voice and leaned over my lap.

Eventually, we made it to the Starboard Inn, though I might've taken the scenic route. Several times. Panting, I threw the car in park and we both bounded toward my room. As I fumbled in my pocket for the room key, Mindy's hands slipped around my waist and crawled up my shirt.

Clothes were flying off even before the door shut behind us.

I was fifteen the first time we had sex. If I can call it that. Thirty seconds of confusion and throbbing awkwardness, brought to an abrupt and sticky end in the back of her truck. By the end of the summer, though, sex had become something entirely different—a refined ritual that strengthened the bond between us. At least, it had for me. Every touch, every kiss—every moment of vulnerable pleasure—crowded out the world. Mindy became the center of my universe, an anchor for my every thought from the moment I woke in the morning to the moment I nodded off at night.

I loved Mindy Thompson. Everything about her.

Almost.

CHAPTER 19

July 12, 2018 … 11:50 p.m.

Her fingertips brushed against my back, sending goosebumps up my spine. I turned to face her in the darkness. As her lips found mine, she pressed against me. My hands slid down to her hips. The lace at her waistline felt thin and insubstantial. My fingers squeezed underneath and followed skin as smooth as silk to the cleft between her legs. Her breath was hot on my neck, just shy of panting. Her hand rubbed against my cock; it grew harder at her touch.

I kissed her neck and trailed down her chest with my tongue. Her breasts—small by her standards, but absolute perfection by mine—heaved at my touch. My mouth lingered on one, then the other. She moaned faintly, her nipples hardening against my tongue.

"Do it," she whispered, and slid out of her panties.

I knew what she wanted. I wanted it, too. I backed under the covers and kissed her stomach, working my way down. My fingers forged ahead, parting a triangle of velvety hair between my fingers. Mindy purred as a finger glided inside, her flesh wet and softer than rose petals. My lips brushed against her inner thigh and kissed a trail into territory that was at once new and distantly familiar. My tongue explored, my lips caressed. My finger stroked the ridges of her insides. She was moaning and panting. I recognized this at the blurry edge of my senses, lost in my own bliss. When she cried out and heaved against my tongue, I realized how close I was.

Mindy groaned and drew me back to her. Guiding me onto my knees, she took me into her mouth. I couldn't hold back anymore, but when I opened my mouth to warn her, it was too late. I gasped and her grip tightened on my hips. She took me deeper and deeper into her mouth until I was spent.

Trembling, I dropped to the bed and snuggled against her until we were nose to nose. "God, I've missed you," she whispered against my cheek, a laugh ringing at the edge of her voice.

I drew her close, marveling as I had done so many times over the years how perfectly we fit against each other, like two halves of an intricate puzzle. My heart ached. I loved this girl more than should be possible. But to say those words would only spoil the moment. So, I brought my lips to hers and kissed her tenderly.

"Yeah, I might've thought about you a few times, too."

Mindy was the first to fall asleep; she breathed steadily beside me in the darkness with her hair fanned across a feather pillow. Keyed up, it was after two before I finally managed to follow suit. As always, the dreams awaited me. Only, this time—after twenty-five years of the same horror, experienced night after night—everything was different.

It was dark with only a sliver of moonlight penetrating the tree cover.

I couldn't breathe. My fingers gouged frantically at my neck, but it was no use. Behind me, outside my field of view, someone grunted with effort, pulling harder and harder on a string around my neck. The silhouette of a man loomed over me, still as the trees around us. I felt the string burn, possibly even cut into my skin. If I could've muttered a sound, I might've cried out in pain. But it was no use; I'd breathed my last. My head hurt as spots began to speckle my view. My periphery narrowed until only a spotlight of the world remained. By instinct alone, I clawed at the hands of my killer, snatched at hair and bare flesh. All to no avail.

Mercifully, the pain faded as darkness drew me into a warm embrace. From a million miles away, a voice whispered into the abyss.

"Did I do it right? Is she dead?"

I bolted upright in bed, dragging the comforter with me. My chest heaved.

Beside me, Mindy roused. "What is it?"

I couldn't respond; the dream hadn't yet released me. Shaky hands examined my neck, feeling for the garrote that had all but crushed my throat only moments ago. I almost sobbed with relief when I found nothing there.

Despite the piss-poor air conditioning, goosebumps flurried up my body.

Mindy flipped on the lamp and laid a hand on my arm. "It's okay, baby," she crooned. "It's just a dream." She scratched my back lightly.

My breathing slowed and I nodded. I reached into a pile of clothes at my bedside and retreated under the covers with a t-shirt.

"What're you doin'?" Mindy muttered.

"I'm cold," I replied, slipping the shirt on with teeth chattering.

"Poor baby," she said softly. "That must've been one hell of a dream."

I moaned in agreement.

"Lie back down," she whispered, patting my pillow. I obeyed, and soon the lamp clicked back off. Deft fingers massaged my scalp as Mindy pressed against me, lending me her blessed warmth. I closed my eyes, the dream already falling apart in my memory.

"Where'd you get that?"

Mindy's voice dragged me from sleep. I sat up and rubbed my eyes, glancing wearily at the clock. Nearly six a.m.

"What's wrong, babe?"

She leveled a trembling finger at the nightstand, where my revolver gleamed in the lamplight. She wore a towel around her torso, her hair hanging in damp clumps down her shoulders.

"Oh, that? A pawn shop. Why?"

Mindy's mouth clamped shut, her eyes wide and haunted. And—unless I was imagining things in my sleepy state—angry.

"Listen, I can put it away." I snatched the hunk of steel by the barrel and shoved it into the nightstand drawer. "See? It's gone."

Her expression remained stricken.

With sleep finally losing its grip, a breakdown in logic vied for my attention. Mindy was the daughter of a sheriff; she'd grown up in a household full of guns. Hell, I'd seen her punch a bullseye at twenty yards with my dad's 1911.

When I took another look at the nightstand, it dawned on me what had filled her with such unease. It wasn't the gun, I realized, but the necklace sprawled beside it. I picked up the beaded strand and dangled it between us.

"You recognize this?" I asked.

"It's mine," she replied with a bit of steel. "You been going through my stuff?"

The blood seemed to cool in my veins. "Of course not. Where'd you get it?"

She hesitated. "I-I... it was a gift." A drop of water dripped from her hair onto the bed with a soft pat.

I let the necklace fall to my lap and brushed her damp shoulder with the back of my hand. "From who?"

She shook her head, sending a few more water droplets onto the bed.

"C'mon, Mindy. Throw me a bone here."

Her eyes opened defiantly, glaring holes through me. "It's got nothing to do with you, Shane."

Holding up the necklace, I shook my head. "I think we both know better than that by now."

"Do we? If either of us has some explaining to do, it's you, Shane. If you didn't go through my things, how'd you get it?"

"My mom had it," I replied, cocking my head. "You didn't give it to her?"

Looking away again, Mindy pursed her lips. "She didn't get it from me."

"Who gave it to you?" I asked for the second time."

"My grandpa. When I was a kid."

CHAPTER 20

May 24, 2000 … 2:05 p.m.

They were trying to get a rise out of me, I knew. The three of them. "She's one hot piece of ass, I'll tell you what. And holy shit, can she suck a dick!"

"Damn right. Did you do her in the ass? I did. She didn't want to at first, but she changed her tune once we got going."

They hadn't spoken her name specifically, but I knew exactly who they were talking about. Everybody talked about Mindy. They had since I could remember. She was the first girl her age to grow boobs, to have her period. And if the rumors were true, she'd lost her virginity long before I'd experienced my first wet dream.

I didn't care. People could say whatever the hell they wanted—God knows they talked enough shit about me. The only thing that mattered was that Mindy and I were together. I loved her and she loved me.

"What about you, Ghost Boy?" one of the guys shouted in my direction. "You tap that ass yet?"

With my mouth clamped shut like a bear trap, I slammed my locker door and headed to fifth-hour Biology. Thanks to the commotion of a few stragglers jogging by from the other direction, I didn't even hear the assholes closing the distance behind me. I was twenty paces from the classroom when they got me.

A hard shove sent me sprawling from behind. I hit the floor hard, my head rebounding like a tether ball off the linoleum. Dazed, I scrambled to my feet in time to catch a right cross to the jaw. I rolled with it and threw a blind punch of my own through a field of stars. I hit something soft but rigid, something that collapsed with a crunch under my knuckles.

The attack ended as quickly as it started. I stumbled into Biology and dropped into an empty desk. Not my desk, I knew on some level, but it would have to do. I cradled my head in shaking hands to wait. The principal would send for me sooner or later, I knew.

He got around to it fifteen minutes into class. My head pounded like never before, but I followed the student aid to the office.

Principal Myers greeted me with a shove in the direction of his office. "Get in there, Gibson."

I fell into an empty chair and gripped the seat edges to keep from falling. The room was spinning mercilessly.

"How'd you think this was gonna play out, dipshit?" the principal was saying. "You put one of your classmates in the hospital and expect to just carry on like nuthin happened?"

I opened my mouth to rebut, but my lunch got there first.

The principal backed away with a grimace as I redecorated his carpet. "Ah, shit. Goddammit, Gibson."

Suddenly the floor was coming at me, puke and all, and I could do nothing to stop it.

I remember coming to in a hospital bed without a clue how I'd gotten there, much less why. My mom was in a chair nearby, her face taut with worry. Her eyes were closed, her hands clasped in her lap.

"Hey, Mom."

Her eyes shot open. "Oh, thank God," she muttered, lurching to her feet. "Don't try to move, okay?"

I nodded, which was immediately rewarded by a stab of pain through my head.

"What's wrong with me?" I hissed.

"You have a concussion."

Fantastic. "What happened?" I had to ask. Seriously—I couldn't remember a damn thing with my head pounding like that, pulsing like a giant hand squeezing the hell out of my brain.

"I was hopin' you could tell me. One of your classmates is across the hall with a ruptured trachea."

I didn't respond.

She closed her eyes and nodded. "I called your dad. He'll be here in a few hours."

"Why? Do I have to... how long do I have to stay here?"

My mom turned toward the window, her mouth now quivering. "You've been expelled, Shane."

"What? But..." My memory returned a few snippets of information—enough to piss me off. "It was three against one!"

Her head snapped back in my direction, her mouth slightly agape. I saw my indignation mirrored in her expression for a second, and then her eyes went half-lidded. With shock, or resignation—hard to distinguish one from the other with my vision going in and out of focus. "Doesn't matter," she sighed bitterly.

"What are we supposed to do?"

"I'm so sorry, Shane. Please know I don't fault you in any of this. But it's clear to me now that this damn town's never gonna give you a fair shake in life." Her head swayed slowly from side to side. "I really thought we'd all get past it," she lamented. "But I was wrong. There's no place for you here."

For me. Not us, just... *me*. "So Dad's taking me with him?"

"Yes."

The plan was already in motion, I realized; there was no sense trying to fight it. Looking back, I can't help but wonder if I should have. Maybe I was supposed to. But I was tired of fighting, of defending my right to live in peace. Tired of being me, here.

"What about Mindy?"

My mother's eyes hardened. She swallowed, wiped her cheeks dry. "What about her?"

"I can't just... I love her, Mom."

She gave me a pitying frown that was mostly in the eyes. "Shane, you're sixteen. You don't know what love is yet."

I blinked. "Why would you say something like that?"

"Because it's true. You're not in love, Shane. That girl's got you by the libido, and you're too naive to know any better."

My heart ached. I was used to belittlement by my peers, even their parents. But my own mother? It stung like a slap to the face.

She sighed and gazed back out the window, where a flock of Canadian geese was flying in. "I know it seems like the end of the world, believe me. I was a teenager too, you know. But I need you to trust me on this: you'll bounce back."

I wouldn't, though. I knew it in my heart, deep in my gut.

"It's part of the teenage condition," she was saying. "I can re-member when I was your age, I—"

Abruptly, her attention darted to the door and she stiffened.

"Oh. C'mon in, Mindy."

CHAPTER 21

July 13, 2018 … 7:15 a.m.

A car bumped its horn outside, stirring me from sleep. Mindy gave me a peck on the forehead and let herself out. I opened a tired eye in a slit to glance at the clock. A little after seven.

Too damn early.

I pressed into the covers to drift back to sleep. I was almost there when a sound disturbed me. I opened my eyes but remained still.

It was the woman again; she stood motionless at the end of my bed, filthy, dripping muddy water onto the floor. I slid from under the covers and reached into the nightstand drawer for my revolver. I had no plans to shoot her—was there a point in shooting a dead person, after all?—but the gun's heft comforted me.

"What do you want from me?" I asked, getting to my feet with the bed between us.

Her gaze dropped to the floor.

I took a few steps toward her. She crouched slowly to the floor. No—that wasn't right. She wasn't crouching, I realized, but sliding through the carpet.

"Wait!" I pleaded.

She turned to face me then, reaching for me as if I could save her. When all that remained of her was a hand clutching at thin air, I finally mustered the courage to make contact. Only, instead of pulling her up to safety, she pulled me down. I slipped through the carpet into blackness as if the floor wasn't a floor at all, but a muddy sinkhole.

I was under water.

Jesus, I couldn't breathe! Frantically, I tried to surface, but it was no good. Instead of air, my hands met concrete above. I could see, I realized, though only just. Enough to realize that I wasn't alone. The blank faces of four corpses looked upon me—one mummified in a layer of cloudy plastic, the others falling apart in various stages of decay. The bones of a fifth rolled around at my feet. A scream welled up within me, but I stifled it. I glanced frantically behind me and spotted a rectangle of light. I swam for it with all that I had left in me.

When my head broke the surface, I sucked in a massive breath. I tried to crawl from the concrete chamber, but I was too weak. The water burbled below as fingers locked around my ankles and tugged. Another set of hands got me by the shirt. Though I resisted, I didn't have the strength. I slipped back into the water, where death gathered in the depths, licking its chops.

"No!" I wailed, forfeiting a torrent of bubbles.

When I opened my eyes sometime later, it took a minute to be sure I wasn't still dreaming. Instead of lying in bed, I was sprawled on the ground, soaked to the bone. I was dressed in boxers. The faint whisper of waves lapped somewhere nearby. I stumbled to my feet and took a long look around. Mere yards away, I noticed a path meandering through the trees. It, along with the waves, seemed to draw me in, beckoning me as if it knew me by name.

I followed it until the gravel petered out at the water's edge. There, the crumbling remains of a house foundation peeked just above the water line. My pulse thrummed in my ears as I approached it. My t-shirt was there, half submerged at the water's edge.

In the treetops around me, the nervous titter of blackbirds seemed to whisper in the breeze.

My shirt remained wet after squeezing out the water, but I put it on anyway. Standing there in a daze, I took a few seconds to survey the shoreline before heading inland. The path resolved into a gravel road ahead. Following it, the area struck me as vaguely familiar, though I'd never actually seen it from this direction before. Fox Run turned to pavement a few hundred yards upstream, I knew; I could just make out guard rails scaling a hill in the distance. Until now, I'd never even wondered what was at this end of this road. The truth is, I hadn't come anywhere near this area since I was twelve.

Barely half a mile up the road, a gravel path cut through the woods to Yonker's Marina. There, mere yards from the boat ramp, thirty-six children had died.

I footed the winding access road toward the dam, wincing at the hot asphalt and sharp bits of chert underfoot. It dawned on me along the way that this wasn't my first time walking this road. I'd navigated it barefoot once before, but from the other direction.

Thanks to the summer heat, my clothes—however scant—were dry by the time I reached a convenience store. The cashier was kind enough to lend me the phone, despite my disheveled appearance and a 'No Shoes/No Shirt, No Service' sign on the door. Winnie picked me up twenty minutes later.

"What the hell are you doin' out here in your damn underwear?" she demanded with exasperation. "You're filthy!"

I didn't have a good answer, so I shrugged.

"Well, where's your car?"

"Back at the motel, I guess."

"You guess?"

I could only shrug in response.

We drove in silence then, each of us trying to make sense of things from a different angle. She had to be wondering if I'd fallen off my rocker. Again.

When we passed the turnoff to the Starboard Inn, I stiffened. "What're you doing?" I had to ask.

"I'm kidnapping my crazy nephew for lunch."

Back at my mom's house, I showered away the smell of mud and decay and threw on some of my dad's abandoned clothes and a pair of flip-flops. We ate turkey sandwiches, washed down by sweet tea. Glancing around, I couldn't help but notice the place seemed untouched.

"You haven't moved in yet?"

Winnie waved this off. "I'll get around to it eventually." And then, as she was prone to do when a discussion made her uncomfortable, she changed the subject. "We need to get some weed killer down," she informed me. "Your mom used to pay a service, but I had her call 'em off once she got real sick. Bastards were chargin' her fifty bucks a visit. Can you believe that?"

I could. Frankly, I'd rather pay fifty bucks than get my hands dirty, too. Steeling myself for what would undoubtedly be an unwelcome redirect of conversation, I wiped my mouth with a napkin and bit the bullet. "Winnie, I need to ask you something, and I need the truth."

The woman's arms crossed indignantly. "Well, it ain't like I make a habit of lyin' to people, Shane."

"That necklace," I said flatly. "You recognized it. I saw it in your eyes."

Her already-pale cheeks went damn near transparent.

"I need to know."

"No, what you *need* is to drop this, Shane."

"Funny, I've lost count of how many times I've heard that phrase since I got here."

Winnie drained the last of her tea and smacked her lips. "Maybe the universe is tryin' to tell you sumthin."

"It's important, Winn. Please. I need to understand this."

Winnie chewed the inside of one cheek, creating a crater on its otherwise smooth outer surface. "Fine," she muttered, dropping her napkin on her empty plate. "Coupla weeks ago, a group of ladies from First Methodist came by. The whole town probably knew how sick your mom was, by then."

I swallowed and set my jaw. "Go on."

"They stayed for an hour or so, and that was that." She waved a fly off her empty plate. "Anyway, a few days later, I found a cigar box. In your room."

My eyebrows shot up.

"It was prob'ly a day or two after I sent that letter. I figured I'd change your sheets and do a little dustin', and there it was."

A smirk tugged at the corners of my mouth. "You knew I'd come."

She grunted with an endearing hint of familial condescension. "Of course I did, dummy."

"Tell me about the box."

"Found it under your bed. Thing was full of weird shit—locks of hair, earrings. A belt buckle. Necklaces."

"Including the one Mom had?"

Winnie shook her head and slapped a hand to her chest. "Hand to God, Shane—I don't know how she ended up with that. I threw that damn box away."

I chewed my lip with equal parts curiosity and despair.

"Why would one of those church ladies plant that box in your room?" Winnie wanted to know.

A perfectly logical explanation unfurled in my mind, but I crumpled it up and cast it away, refusing to acknowledge it. "Wish I knew."

Brian Whitney hadn't aged well. I might not have recognized him if not for a birthmark on his cheek—an embellishment that had given him a bad-boy appeal as a teenager, but now only served to highlight his uneven pallor. He recognized me immediately, which was no surprise.

"Help you?" he asked with a neutral expression. He was organizing boxes of drywall screws into neat rows on a metal shelf, the aisle crowded with shrink-wrapped pallets of new inventory.

"Looking for some weed killer."

He rose and strode across the hardware store. I followed dutifully. "Bermuda or Fescue?" he asked over his shoulder.

"Hell if I know. Hard to tell with all the clover and crabgrass."

"Johnson grass, too?"

"Yep."

He stopped before a pallet of twenty-pound bags, then moved on to another. "Here we go. This should do the trick. Just be sure to water it in the day after you put it down."

"Perfect."

He turned to regard me more directly, his hands clasped across his beltline. "Anything else?"

"No, that should do it. Thanks." I scooped up two bags and turned to leave.

"Hey, Shane."

I stopped and swiveled on the balls of my feet.

Brian cleared his throat. "Listen, I just wanted to, uh... you know. Apologize."

Taken aback, I gawked in response.

"For pickin' on you, I mean." Pink spots bloomed on his cheeks. "Been wantin' to tell you that for a long time. I was a real... well, you know. So... I'm real sorry for that."

I was about to reply when, with a curt nod, he excused himself. I mumbled a bewildered *thank you* and headed for the front register.

I used Dad's old spreader to put down the weed killer. It couldn't have taken more than thirty minutes, but the humidity seemed to add hours to the experience. When I was finished, I downed two glasses of water, back to back, and headed to my old bedroom to lay down. I don't remember closing my eyes, but I must have.

One needs to be asleep to dream, after all.

Up until last night, I'd been more or less used to the dreams. It was a bit like watching the same gory movie, night after night. But like last night's, this dream was different.

It was dark, but the moon was sufficient to illuminate my path along the shore. A breeze whispered through the trees, billowing a yellow sundress against my knees. I was angry, but I couldn't remember why. Up ahead, an enclosed fishing dock creaked to and fro, jostled by the wind and waves. The word *Yonker's* spanned the length of the structure in bold script.

Some fifty feet from shore, a low moaning came from the woods. Moments later, it sounded again, this time with a higher pitch. Curiosity drew me between sycamores and oaks into a ravine. There, a man lay on a blanket with a woman straddling him; she rocked and occasionally moaned with pleasure.

Cheeks flushing, I headed back to shore. From the ravine, a voice called out. "Hey!" Footsteps approached.

"I'm so sorry," I said, skin crawling with embarrassment. "I didn't realize—"

My words dissolved into surprise as the man stepped into a puddle of moonlight. I knew him. I couldn't put a name to the face, but I definitely knew him.

"Well, hey there, stranger," he said. He was buckling his pants with a nervous chuckle as he neared me.

"I didn't see a thing," I assured him with a nervous laugh. "Your secret is safe with me."

I was half a second from rushing away when I saw her. She stood in the mouth of the ravine, naked and completely unabashed. I couldn't make out her face, but she couldn't have been more than twelve or thirteen. Probably younger.

The man lunged for me. In a split second, he had me by the hair and throat, dragging me into the shadows of the ravine. I tripped and landed on my back.

"Don't you start screamin', you hear me?"

The man bent over to untie one of his boots, yanking the string free. "You wanna give it a shot this time?"

The girl, who had settled onto the ground behind me, squealed with delight. "Seriously?"

I sensed his grin more than I saw it, given the darkness. I knew I should at least try to run, but I was too petrified to move. He tossed the string to the girl and gave her a nod. "Go on, now."

At once, the string slipped around my throat and pulled taut. As it cinched tighter and tighter, I tried to scream, but nothing came out. When I tried to rise and roll away, the man pressed me back into the dirt under a heavy boot. Behind me, the girl grunted with effort.

"You got it," the man offered encouragingly. "That's my girl."

Abruptly, he crouched beside me and shook me by the shoulders. His features swam in and out of focus. "Wake up!" he growled. "Wake up, goddammit!"

I sat upright with a start, gasping for breath.

"Jesus, that must've been one hell of a dream," Winnie remarked with a disconcerted expression.

I breathed in great gulps, trying to grab at pieces of the dream before they dissolved into nothing.

Winnie patted me on the shoulder with concern. "You were screamin'. Heard it all the way from the RV."

"Sorry, Winnie. I-I'm good now."

She frowned. "Does this happen a lot, Shane? Nightmares, I mean?"

"Nah," I lied, my breathing now under control. I rose from the bed and stretched. "You mind taking me back to the motel?"

With concern etched into her face, my aunt nodded.

I was in much better shape by the time I returned to my room. My phone was on the nightstand, exactly where I'd left it. Two missed calls and a text message. The text was from my buddy, Adam.

When are you coming home?!?

I replied as honestly as I could. *No idea. Will keep you posted.*

Both missed calls were from Rubicon Manufacturing, my employer. I listened to the voicemail with a knot growing in my stomach.

"Hey, Shane. It's Devon—" Devon, being my supervisor. *"—Just touching base. I scheduled you off for this week like we talked about, but it's Friday now, and I kinda thought I'd hear from you before the weekend. Give me a shout and let me know how things are looking. I've got you on the schedule for Monday morning. I, uh... I really need to hear from you*

if that's not gonna work, Shane."

I deleted the message on my way out to the car and headed to the library. I had too much on my mind to worry about Devon and his stupid schedule.

The man from the dream—it had to be Sheriff Thompson. I hadn't recognized the girl, but I—rather, the victim—had known the man, even if she couldn't identify him for certain. It was strange to share thoughts with someone in a dream; lately, it was becoming difficult to distinguish the line where one ceased to be the other.

I was useless on a computer for anything beyond a basic Google search. Thankfully, I had Jean to lean on. She went to work with admirable vigor.

"You remember the toilet that was backed up?" she asked idly.

Clackety-clack, went the keyboard.

"Nope," I replied. "No idea what you're talking about." Hard to forget, really; the odor still lingered faintly as if it had seeped into the pages of a thousand books.

She skewered me with an annoyed glance, then turned her attention back to the computer.

"It was a sock. Who the hell flushes a sock down the toilet?"

I shook my head at the shame of it. "What can I say? Guys are gross." I didn't bother to mention some of the horror shows I'd seen in public restrooms; she'd probably never eat again.

"You sure are." She pecked away at her keyboard with expert precision, emitting a strained sigh of frustration now and then. "I don't know, Shane," she finally relented. "It's hard to find much without some kind of time parameters."

It hit me then. "When did Yonker's put that fishing dock in, do you remember? The enclosed one."

Jean thought for a moment. "Hmm. Seems like 1991? Maybe '92?"

"Let's go back to '90 just to be safe."

"Will do. I doubt she was a local, though," she pointed out. "I mean, it would be common knowledge if she was. Women don't just disappear from a town this small without shit hitting the fan."

She had a point. "Maybe not from Langley, but what about the rest of the county? Not to mention neighboring counties."

"True. I'll add in Craig and Delaware counties while I'm at it." She performed a few more queries and finally perked up. "Here we go. Looks like fifty-nine pending disappearances in the area, dating back to 1990." She scrolled soberly through the search results. "Thirty-three were female. All but twelve were reported in the last decade. Mostly high-school girls, from what I can tell. Probably runaways."

"Well, that narrows things down a bit."

Jean frowned. "The older reports don't have photos on file."

"Well, shit."

"Technology was pretty lackluster back then. They probably didn't have the means to scan and upload photos. Hell, I'm not even sure the internet was around back then."

Made sense. "What are their names?"

"Well, let's see. Penny Wheeler from Pryor. Patricia Crofut from Spavinaw. Stella Whitehorse from Bernice. Kelly—"

"Wait—did you say Whitehorse?"

"Uh-huh." Jean's eyes widened. "Oh, shit. Look at the filing date, Shane."

I did and felt my mouth go dry. "I think we better pay Carl a visit."

Jean glanced at a clock on the wall. "I'm not off until eight. Do you need me there?"

It's hard to say why, in retrospect, but I did indeed need her with me. The thought of facing Carl alone seemed more daunting than I cared to admit. On the other hand, eight seemed a little late to barge in on the old man. He'd probably be in bed by then—assuming the geriatric stereotype of dinner-at-five, bed-at-six held any water.

"Is Rhea coming in today? Maybe she can cover for you."

"Nope," Jean replied with a frown. "Off for the rest of the week. Not that I could leave her in charge, anyway."

"Shit. What time do you work tomorrow?"

A corner of her mouth crept up her cheek. "I don't. As it happens, we're closed on weekends."

"Perfect."

The History Channel was airing back-to-back episodes of The Curse of Oak Island, a documentary that appeared to chronical the systematic—and exorbitantly expensive—destruction of a poor, defenseless island in search of buttons and old coins too worn to pay for themselves.

Winnie called just as I was nodding off. "You hungry?"

"When am I not?"

She blew a raspberry. "You're so damn skinny, I figured you were on a keto diet or sumthin."

I turned the TV off with a crooked grin. "Depends. Is that the one where you eat whatever the hell you want and burn off the calories with pure anxiety?"

"Is that what you're doin'? Get on over here and let me cook you a steak."

I considered bowing out—I was indeed hungry, but I was really hoping to have a talk with Mindy. I hated the secrecy between us; I felt it festering like a canker sore. We needed to clear the air.

In the end—which is to say, when Mindy didn't return my calls or text messages—I headed over to see Winnie, stopping for an oversized bottle of cabernet on the way. The bottle was half gone before the steaks even hit the grill.

"Slow down, Shane," she chided. "The night is young."

She was right, of course. I needed to put on the brakes. The problem was, I needed desperately to lose myself in something. A marathon roll in the hay with Mindy, a bottle of vodka; a bare-knuckled brawl with a few of Langley's finest—it didn't matter much. Anything to be someone else, to disconnect from reality for a while.

As it turned out, Winnie had just the ticket.

"Found these in your mom's closet," she said reverently. "Thought you ought to have them."

She handed over a shoebox crammed with family photos. Old Polaroids of my parents before I was born, five-by-seven snapshots of neighborhood cookouts studded with faces I couldn't place, wedding photos, baby pictures, you name it. Documented proof that life had once been a happy affair for the Gibsons, back before the world turned to shit.

We ate ribeyes and finished off the wine, Winnie offering patient commentary about each photo along the way. Her cheeks were rosy, her smile more relaxed than I'd seen it in a long while. When we finished our stroll down memory lane, she closed the box and clasped her hands on the table before her. She licked her lips nervously.

"So, I, uh… I sorta met someone," she said.

My eyebrows hiked up the slope of my forehead. "Oh yeah?"

She hesitated. "Her name's Melinda."

"Where'd you meet her?"

Winnie rolled her lips and covered her mouth to hide a smile that simply wouldn't be denied. "Online."

"What, like a dating site?"

"Sumthin like that."

Her cheeks—rosy only moments ago—had turned crimson. My first instinct was to give her a hard time like I would with anything else, but something held me back. Did she expect me to burst from my chair in disgust? To cut all ties with her? God, I hoped not. When her eyes glassed over, I took her hand.

"That's great, Winn," I said. "Really."

The relief in her expression was hard to overlook. That she'd been afraid to be herself around me for all these years, and that she honestly didn't think I already knew—it broke my heart a little. "So when do I get to meet her?"

My aunt laughed and gave my hand a squeeze. "Hard to say," she replied. "She lives in Eureka Springs, so it'll take some plannin'."

"Eureka Springs, huh?" I couldn't hide my smirk. "Does she have dreadlocks?"

"No."

"Does she sell CBD oil and make her own soap?"

Winnie tried and failed to frown. "God, I hope not."

Grinning, I leaned back in my chair. "I'm happy for you, Winn. You've been alone too long."

She wiped her eyes and ran her fingers through her hair. "I have, haven't I?"

"You did that for mom's sake?"

Winnie looked at me for a long moment, trying to frame a careful response. She didn't need to, though. I knew how it was.

"Mom loved you, Winn. No matter what."

She nodded, but her smile was gone. "She cried a lot near the end, you know. Said she feared for my eternal soul."

An empathetic sigh hissed through my teeth. "Her heart was in the right place."

"Was it?" Winnie turned away bitterly. "She treated me like some kind of a pervert sometimes. Hell, I've never even been with a man, much less a woman. But I guess the attraction alone's gonna send me to hell, either way." She sniffled and tried to smile. "Like I can help it."

I couldn't imagine a life without intimacy, without connecting with someone physically. The injustice of her self-denial cut through me. I wanted to cry for Winnie, as if that would do any good.

It hit me then, without an ounce of satisfaction; this must've been what kept Winnie in that RV for all these years. Ever since I could remember, she and my mom had kept up a strange sort of diplomatic dance, one that allowed each to tolerate the other with the caveat that neither would ever know the other with any real depth.

For the first time, I think I understood why.

Still, I had to wonder: had Mom given her own sister the boot when the truth emerged, or had Winnie moved out of her own volition?

"Doesn't matter anymore," I pointed out, to myself as much as Winnie. "She's gone. And you're stuck with me." I patted the back of her hand affectionately. "Now, I'm gonna need to see some pictures of this, uh—Miranda?"

"Melinda."

"That's what I said. I wonder if she makes her own clothes out of hemp."

Winnie shook her head, trying to stifle a smirk. "God, I'm glad you're home again."

July 14, 2018 … 8:48 a.m.

Carl was poking into the crawlspace under his mobile home with a broom handle when we pulled up his driveway.

"Damn varmint under there," he grumbled. "Hope it ain't a skunk." He laughed genially and leaned the broom against the trailer.

He gave Jean a hug, a warm handshake for me.

"Rhea sure loves workin' with you at the library, Jean," he said. "She talks about it all the time."

Jean beamed. "She's a great kid, and I'm happy to have her." She offered a goofy frown. "Just wish I could pay her!"

They both laughed. I tried to smile along, but I was feeling a little out of sorts.

We followed Carl inside, out of the heat—seriously, Oklahoma: ninety-two degrees before nine a.m.? He offered us sweet tea, but we both declined. He sat in his recliner and motioned for us to hold down the couch.

"So to what do I owe the pleasure?" he asked.

Jean took the lead. "We stumbled across something yesterday that got us pretty curious. We're hoping you might be able to help."

Carl offered a toothless grin. "Well, I'll sure give it a shot."

"It's about Stella," I added.

The grin fell away like a rock.

"Why didn't you mention your wife's disappearance?" I asked. It took concentrated effort to keep my irritation from surfacing. I had to remind myself that Carl Whitehorse was a victim.

The old man crossed his arms and leaned back into his chair. "You didn't ask."

Jean cleared her throat, a subtle but clear warning to back off. I let her take the baton. "Mr. Whitehorse, can you tell us about your wife?"

He frowned. "Not much to tell no more. We were married for twenty-seven years. One day, she up and left. Never saw her again."

"It wasn't just any day, was it?" I tried to clarify.

Carl leveled a tired gaze on me. "No, it sure wasn't."

I chewed my lip. "You filed a missing person's report."

The old man nodded sheepishly. "It hit me real hard when she took off. Came out of nowhere, y'understand. I wouldn't even consider she mighta left willingly, 'specially with the drownin' and all."

Jean shot me a sidelong glance, then smiled faintly at the old man. "Did you two argue the day she left?"

Carl bobbed his head yes and no, tried to smile. "Prob'ly. When you've been married as long as we were, you argue most days." He shrugged. "She'd usually go walk it off somewhere and we'd make up later."

"Where would she go?" Jean wanted to know. "Did she have a favorite place to cool down?"

"Depended on how mad she was. She'd walk down to the pond, most times. It's just down the hill." He nodded out the window with an unshaven chin. "Sometimes she'd drive out to the lake."

"Did you look for her after she left?" I wanted to know.

"'Course. I asked around town, called her sister in Tulsa. Come t'find out, Stella left me for a younger man. A *white* man."

My eyebrows rose. "Her sister told you that?"

"No, no. There was an investigation."

Jean perked up. "Oh, yeah?"

"Me and Sheriff Thompson don't see eye to eye on many things, but he did me right where Stella was concerned. If not for Jim, I'd never know what b'came of her." He cleared his throat. "The mind conjures terrible images in a vacuum. I'm grateful to have some closure."

"Would it surprise you to learn she's still listed as missing?"

Carl squinted dubiously, but then shrugged. "Not really. Everything was done on paper, back then. A form prob'ly got misplaced or sumthin."

I rose and wandered across the living room to a patch of photos on the wall. My breath snagged at the back of my throat when I saw her, posed in full color. Stella's eyes were dark, but soft and kind; her complexion, the color of tanned deer hide. The image of her in my motel room—skin drained of all pigment, eyes as cold and black as death itself—crept into the periphery of my thoughts.

"Did she own a yellow sundress?" I asked without thinking. The moment the words passed my lips, I realized that I'd misspoken. A quick glance over my shoulder told me there was no un-ringing that bell.

Jean paled, closed her eyes.

Carl cocked his head for a second, then went rigid in his chair. His head swiveled from me to Jean, and then back again. His gnarled hands gripped the upholstered arms of his chair for all he was worth. "What's this about, you two? Has sumthin happened to Stella?"

My first instinct was to backpedal. "I apologize, Carl. I just meant—"

"Tell me what's goin' on, by God," he growled.

Jean swore under her breath, shaking her head. *Don't you dare,* her eyes seemed to say.

I should've heeded her warning. I should've left the truth dead and buried, where it couldn't hurt a living soul again.

I know that now.

I approached the old man and dropped to one knee at the foot of his chair. "Do you remember what you told me the last time I was here, Carl?"

The old Indian blinked in response, his eyes wild with uncertainty.

"You told me the truth gets ugly, but that doesn't make it any less important."

Tears sprang to his eyes. His expression wasn't merely worried, I realized; it was fractured. I wondered if, on some level, he knew she was dead. Perhaps he'd known all along. "She's... oh, Jesus. What happened?"

So I told him. God forgive me, I told him every damn word.

CHAPTER 22

July 14, 2018 … 10:17 a.m.

I was learning all about giant squids on the Discovery Channel—in color!—when someone knocked on my door. I threw on a t-shirt and opened the door a crack. Outside, a kid in his twenties darkened my doorway.

"Help you?"

"Biggun wants to see you."

"Uh, who's that?"

"Biggun."

I leaned against the door jam. "I don't have the slightest idea who that is. But hey, did you know a giant squid's eye can grow the size of a basketball?"

The kid gave me a blank stare. "Let's go, asshole."

I gave my chin a bored scratch. "Hmm. I'm not too keen on

riding with strangers. What's your name?"

"They call me Slip."

I tried to keep a straight face, but I doubt I came even close. "Slip," I parroted with exaggerated annunciation. "They call you that, and you just, like… let 'em get away with it?"

The kid bucked up on me, pushing me inside. "Don't nobody disrespect me like that, man."

I threw up my hands plaintively. "Listen, you're disrespecting yourself with a name like that. I'm just trying to help you."

His jaw clenched, but he backed off. "Whatever, bitch. Let's go. Biggun's waitin'."

I could've sent him on his way—not to be conceited, but you get a feel for who you can own in a fight, and this guy didn't stand a chance. He must've intuited my thoughts because he raised his shirt to reveal a gun in his waistband. Mine was in the nightstand drawer, where it did me absolutely no good.

Sigh.

"Okay, Slip. You win. But you're buying breakfast."

Slip drove me to an abandoned barbeque joint on the edge of town and parked around back. I followed him inside with a mild sense of foreboding. I could handle Slip, but who knew what await-ed me in there?

A rack of dried-out spareribs?

A shriveled-up rope of hotlinks?

A moldy lump of congealed brisket?

I shivered at the thought.

Four guys were waiting inside. Among them was my good old friend, Kenny. I gave him an affectionate wink. "How's the foot?"

The kid's eyes hardened and flicked to an enormous man in overalls. Fat rolls spilled between his armholes and shoulder straps. Despite his size, he had a baby face with a wispy goatee. He couldn't have been more than twenty-five.

"You must be Biggun," I remarked, because one of us had to break the ice.

"And you must be batshit crazy," he snapped in reply.

"I've been called worse," I confided with a crooked smile. "So what can I do for you?"

Two of his men peeled off the group and flanked me on each side, leaving me vulnerable at the center of a circle. Biggun took a step toward me but kept a good yard between us.

"Heard you was messin' with my boy."

I stole a glance at Kenny; arms crossed, the kid wore a satisfied smirk.

My eyebrows shot up. "Kenny's your boy? Jesus, how old were you when he was born? Seven, eight?"

"So you're a comedian," Biggun glowered, his flabby arms now folded across a midriff the size of a truck tire.

I waved this off. "Nah, I'm not a professional. I do a pretty mean mime impression, though. Check this out." I planted my hands against an invisible barrier and put on a theatric frown, patting my hands up and down the imaginary wall.

"Cut it out," Biggun groaned, eyes rolling like a teenage girl.

I pretended the wall was closing in on me, mouthing, "Oh, no!" with a hand on one cheek.

"Stop it, asshole."

Sigh. Some people have no appreciation for the arts. I allowed my expression to harden a bit. "How'd you think this was gonna play out, man? You drag me in here looking like a gangsta moonshiner and I'm supposed to cower in fear?"

Biggun gave one of his guys a faint nod. A fist dove into my kidney from behind, rocking my tender ribs and sending a wave of searing pain through my entire body. Slip leaned against the wall and snickered.

"You were sayin'?" Biggun drawled.

I gasped between clenched teeth, doing my best to stay standing. Kenny howled and clapped his hands, drawing a scornful glare from his boss.

When I could breathe properly again, I dared to speak. "I asked Kenny not to sell drugs to my girlfriend. If you wanna call that *messin' with your boy*, I guess I'm guilty as charged."

All eyes flicked to Kenny. "That right?" Biggun muttered.

"This bitch practically broke my foot," Kenny protested.

"In fairness," I pointed out, "you did pull a knife on me."

"You're lucky I didn't—"

"Shut the hell up," Biggun snapped. "Both y'all need to zip it."

Kenny huffed and balled his fists at his side, but he complied.

To me, Biggun said, "You think you get to decide who we sell to? You must be trippin', fool."

Jesus, the contrived gangsta vernacular was getting thicker in here by the second. Naturally, I had to join the fun. "How 'bout I ask your momma tonight, right 'fore I kick her fat ass out?"

I know, I know—poking the bear and all that. But these guys were just begging for it.

One of Biggun's crew squealed an, "Oh, shit!" behind me. The big man himself held me in a deadpan gaze, then nodded again to the guy behind me.

Waiting for another blow, I leaned forward an inch. "You've got a flaw in your whole approach, you know."

"Oh, yeah? Why don't you enlighten me?"

"Intimidation only works on someone who gives a shit if he lives or dies." I waited for the blow, but it didn't come. "You know who I am, don't you?" I asked.

Biggun chewed his lip thoughtfully. "Think maybe I've heard of you."

"Then you must know I don't have much going for me. Do whatever the hell you want, I don't give a shit."

Another blow struck me, this one to the side of the head. It hurt, but it lacked the steam I was expecting. For whatever reason, the guy behind me was pulling his punches.

"Who's the girl?" Biggun wanted to know.

I held my tongue, but Kenny spoke up in my stead. "You know, that fine-ass ho from the grocery sto'?"

Biggun's eyes widened. "You better be shittin' me, boy."

Kenny frowned nervously. "Nah, man. What's the problem?"

"Her dad's the Mayes County Sheriff, dumbass," I pointed out helpfully.

Kenny went pale. "How was I supposed to know? She approached *me*, man."

"In his defense," I interjected, "she probably did. She's trying to stay clean, but you know how that goes."

Biggun sighed and lit a Marlboro. "Don't really matter. We're protected."

I let that sink in for a moment. It made sense. A drug operation of any variety didn't stand a chance at longevity in a small town without greasing some palms.

"The sheriff's on your payroll?"

Biggun smirked. "Don't worry your pretty little head about that, boy. You got bigger problems to work out."

I didn't like the sound of that.

The fat man turned to Kenny. "How much did you sell her?"

Kenny swallowed, his Adam's apple sliding up and down his throat. "Like, a gram."

Biggun nodded, his eyebrows scrunched into hairy fat rolls. "A gram. That might get her through the day." He turned to me. "A gram goes for one fifteen, one twenty-five. Prob'ly less in the big city, but out here, the good shit ain't as easy to come by." He plucked a cellphone from the chest pocket of his overalls, swiping it awake with a thick finger. "See, the way I figure it, you're askin' us to give up a minimum of 115 bucks a day over your girl. You willin' to take on that debt?"

"Sounds more like counting chickens than a debt."

"Call it opportunity cost, then. Call it whatever the hell you want, but that's the price for walkin' out of here."

Well, shit. "I'm not exactly made of money," I pointed out. "I can probably cover a few days, but that's it."

Abruptly, Biggun grinned, sporting a mouthful of crooked teeth. "Oh, I got a better idea than that," he cackled. "You're gonna square up, my man. You'll see."

Slip dropped me off at my motel without a word. I didn't bother going in. I was starving. It was just shy of noon by the time I reached Sonic. The place would be hopping soon, but for the moment, business was slow. I ordered a burger and tots. I was hungry enough to eat it right there, but I was becoming more and more apprehensive about doing anything in public lately.

My phone vibrated in my pocket on the way back to the motel. I teased it free and stole a glance at the screen. It was Mike. I was about to answer the call when something occurred to me. I let Mike's call go to voicemail and pulled over to dial another number. My stomach growled impatiently.

The phone rang four times before she picked up. "Hello?" she muttered wearily.

"Mrs. Thompson, it's Shane."

She didn't speak right away, but I could hear her breathing. "Shane, I'm afraid you caught me at a bad time," she finally managed. "I'm running late for a prayer vigil at—"

"You tried to tell me something the other day," I interjected, swatting her paltry objection aside like a gnat. "It didn't sink in until just now."

"I'm not sure what you mean, Shane."

"You said your husband changed even before Carrie died."

She didn't respond and I took her silence to be confirmation. "What changed?"

There was a rustle of fabric against fabric. "You need to quit picking at scabs, Shane. For your own good. And the good of the town."

"Please, Alice. Tell me what you meant. I think it might be important."

She groaned in protest and for a moment I thought she was going to hang up. But she didn't. "He disappeared a lot, came home at all hours smelling like sweat and mischief. I suspected another woman for a while. It made sense at the time."

"But it was something else, wasn't it?"

The old woman didn't respond. She remained silent for so long, in fact, I thought I might've dropped the call. "Alice? Are you still there?"

She cleared her throat. "I'm here, Shane. I've got a casserole in the oven, though. I really need to—"

"You knew, didn't you?" I prodded. "What he was doing?"

A pained sigh. "I suspected."

"Did you tell anyone?"

She chuffed. "Who was I supposed to tell, Shane? My husband was the law. Listen, people either love or hate Jim, but no one in their right mind dares to cross him."

"I'm not judging you, Alice. Please, don't misunderstand. I can't even imagine being in your shoes."

She clicked her tongue. "Yes, well I could say the same for yours."

"How many do you think he killed?"

The line went quiet for three long seconds, and then a sob strangled the silence. "I don't know," she squeaked. "I was just... I was just glad to not be one of 'em. I know that makes me a coward."

"It makes you human."

"Maybe I could've done sumthin," she sniffled. "How many women died b'cause I was too 'fraid to step forward?"

I had no answer to this question. "You did what you had to do to survive. To protect your kids."

"Hell of a lot of good that did."

My heart swelled with empathy. "I love your daughter, you know."

"I know you do, Shane."

"She's here now because of you. She's alive because you stuck around to protect her."

Alice scoffed, sniffling. "Think you've got the wrong idea, Shane. Mindy's daddy would never hurt her."

I wasn't so sure, but it seemed rude to argue. I changed the subject. "What's his connection to Alan Proctor?"

The question seemed to catch her off guard. She sniffled, followed by a thin titter. "You mean Mindy never mentioned him?"

"No, ma'am."

"Well, he's been dead a long while. I s'pose she doesn't want to revisit the memory. Mindy loved that man to pieces. Practically worshipped the ground he walked on."

"How long's it been?" I wanted to know. "Since he passed away, I mean."

"Oh, fifteen years, give or take. You were long gone by then. Anyway, Alan was Jim's stepdaddy."

Suddenly, as if a cog had just slipped into proper alignment within a great machine, it all made sense. I'd allowed the disparity between their last names—Thompson and Proctor—to throw me.

"Truth is," Alice was saying, "Alan passin' away wasn't such a terrible thing. Jim always treated him with respect, but he was never at peace with the man around. Gave me the willies, too, if I'm bein' completely honest."

"But not Mindy."

"Oh, no."

"They spent a lot of time together?"

Alice cleared her throat, suddenly wary. "Just what're you getting' at, Shane?"

"Nothing, sorry. I just…" In mid-thought, a realization struck me hard. Alice Thompson went to church, most likely First Methodist. She'd even mentioned visiting my mother before she passed.

My heart sagged in my chest.

It was her, I realized; I'd suspected it before, but didn't want to believe it. Alice Thompson had planted that cigar box in my room. The implications swirled in my head, moving too quickly and erratically to grasp. Trying like hell to suppress the tremor in my voice, I bit back the accusation.

"Shane?" Alice said. "My casserole's gonna burn. I better go."

I opened my mouth to speak, but there were no words left. Not that it mattered, considering the line had gone dead.

CHAPTER 23

I called Mike back without listening to his voicemail. He answered on the second ring.

"Hey, Shane. Where are you?"

"Headed to my room with some grub. Why? What's up?"

"Listen, you should come over tonight. Crash here, you know?"

"I'll be fine, man."

From nowhere, a tow truck pulled out in front of me with a dog sliding around on the bed. I hit the brakes to keep from rear-ending him and my lunch bag slid off the passenger seat, launching a volley of tater tots onto the floor.

Dammit.

Mike's voice lowered and I could imagine his coworkers sitting nearby, giving him the stink-eye for colluding with the enemy. "I wouldn't be so sure, man. There's been some talk."

"What kind of talk?"

The tow truck slowed to make a turn, taking his sweet time to get out of the way. A grimy decal with the words *Tanner's Tow & Salvage* hung cockeyed from the bumper.

"Nuthin good, brother," Mike was saying. "You need to split or hole up someplace where no one knows to look for you."

"Thanks for the heads up, Mike. Really."

"So you'll crash here?"

"Actually, I've got plans. Rain check?"

Mike was quiet for a long moment. "Be careful, man. I've got a bad feelin'."

My tummy was six tater tots shy of happy, thanks to Tanner's Towing; the rest of me was a wreck. I'd put it off for as long as I could. Pieces of the puzzle were tickling edge against edge, begging to be snapped into place. I didn't want to. I'd already seen glimpses of the larger picture, and what I saw cut like a dull knife.

Alice Thompson had planted the box in my room, that much seemed certain. Its contents weren't merely trinkets, they were mementos—trophies collected from a long string of victims. The part I couldn't work out—at least, the most salient question—was *why*. What could motivate a woman who had always shown me kindness to do something so slimy—to set me up for the sake of protecting her psycho ex-husband, at that?

And what was the point, anyway? Had she planned to call the cops with an anonymous tip? If so, the plan must've fallen apart for her the minute I checked into the Starboard Inn. Was it her, I had to wonder, who'd attempted to have me kicked out of the motel? It made sense. Where else could I have gone then, except to my Mom's?

Dammit.

Not that it would've mattered. The cops wouldn't care if that box was discovered in my old bedroom or my motel room. It was a trivial detail that did nothing to exonerate me.

I had some time to kill before Mindy got off work. Feeling restless, I stopped by a convenience store to fill up the rental. Funny how sometimes you just know things are about to go sideways, even before you realize what's wrong. That was the feeling I got when I wandered inside for a fountain drink. I glanced around suspiciously as I fumbled with a lid, and then a straw. Something felt off, even if I couldn't put my finger on what.

As far as I could see, there was only one other customer in there—an old lady collecting her change for a handful of lottery tickets. As I approached the register though, the door swung open, dinging a brass bell over the door frame.

The cashier glanced over my shoulder and smiled. "Hey, Jackson."

"Hey there, Cassie," came a deep reply.

A glance over my shoulder found a man built like a tank lumbering by.

"The hell you lookin' at, Ghost Boy?" he demanded, stopping in his tracks. It took less than a second to size him up. Muscles on top of muscles, knuckles like peen hammers, cauliflower ears. Scars over both eyebrows. This guy was a brawler, and he was fully equipped to mop the floor with me.

Cassie—a twenty-something redhead with tattoos up both arms—stiffened behind the register. "Cool it, Jackson. Can't have that in the store."

The man leaned in, bumping me from behind. "I'll see you later," he said.

Cassie slapped the counter. "I mean it, Jackson!"

He grumbled something unintelligible but wandered off.

"Sorry about that," she said. Her eyes settled on mine and the corners of her mouth curled up. "Dollar fourteen."

I set my cup on the counter and dug two dollar bills from my pocket.

"So you're the notorious Shane Gibson."

I rewarded this with a flat smile and tossed the bills on the counter. "Yep. Yay me."

She giggled and punched some buttons on the register.

"Keep the change," I said.

"Whatever you say, big spender."

I smiled and turned to leave.

"Wait."

I hesitated near the door with the straw an inch from my lips.

"I get off in an hour, if you're... you know. Bored or whatever."

Well, this was unexpected. "Oh. Um, good to know."

She stuck out her lower lip in a pout.

My cheeks burned. "Sorry, it's just… I'm seeing someone."

Her smile skewed to one side. "So?"

"Wouldn't you prefer a guy who isn't the town pariah?"

She snickered. "Maybe I'm not a fan of small-town convention."

I sipped my drink and gave her a faint nod. "Have a good night, Cassie."

My step faltered just outside. Parked at a pump two rows down from mine was a Jack's Plumbing truck.

"Son of a bitch," I grumbled under my breath.

Just as I was approaching my car, a man pulled up to the pump across from me with a bass boat in tow. Once his gas was pumping, he pilfered around in the back of his boat. Glancing around, his attention settled on the trash can at the end of my pump row.

"Might wanna keep your distance from this, fella," he said with a cringing smile. He dragged a plastic bag bulging with fish guts across the pavement and heaved it into the trashcan. The odor was overwhelming.

"Yikes, you weren't kidding," I gagged.

He shrugged and made a hasty retreat back to his boat, where he busied himself with rearranging fishing poles and coolers. My gaze shot to Jackson's truck and back to the trash can.

Okay, cut me some slack. I mean, what was I supposed to do? The universe was clearly daring me. And I never backed down from a dare.

When the dirty deed was done, I headed across town to the liquor store for a few bottles of wine, smiling all the way; I figured if I was going to hunker down for the night all by my lonesome, I might as well try to enjoy it.

But then, as I trundled back to the car with two bottles of cheap Riesling, I suddenly froze. An elderly man in a beat-up Camry was parked three spots down from me. He looked familiar. Too familiar.

Admittedly, Langley was a small town. But I'd crossed paths with this guy too many times for comfort. First, at Mo's Café—the day after I came into town, I recalled. Later at the public library. And now, here.

With a blank expression, I tossed the wine into my back seat and moseyed over to the Camry. His window came to life at my approach; it was all the way down when I reached him.

"Afternoon," I said.

"Yep."

I scrutinized his face, trying to place him. He had no identifying features, save for a faint but wide scar on his upper lip—the lingering fingerprint of a cleft palate. A memory toyed with the edge of my thoughts, but I just couldn't catch it.

"I know you," I muttered. "Can't remember how, though."

The man nodded. "Long time ago."

I shoved my hands into my pockets. "Throw me a bone, would you?" I asked, kindly but firmly.

"Name's Lloyd Spence."

The name did nothing for me.

"You'd prob'ly remember me better as *Deputy* Spence."

I closed my eyes and smiled faintly when I finally snagged a memory. The smile faded abruptly though, because it wasn't the kind of memory I liked to revisit. "You were one of the deputies who interrogated me the day of the drowning. You and Jim Thompson."

A slow nod and a sniff.

I let my gaze wander over his worn-out clothes and modest car—easily fifteen years old. "I take it you didn't retire with a pension."

"Nope." A bland smile.

"Mr. Spence, is there something you'd like to tell me?"

He shrugged indifferently.

"You left a photo on my car."

He neither confirmed nor denied this; rather, he put an elbow out the window and slapped the door. "How 'bout we take a little ride?"

We drove past the dam and continued northeast for several miles. Along the way, Lloyd didn't give up a single word that I didn't pull from him. It got old pretty quickly.

"I feel like I'm doing all the talking. Is there a reason you've been following me around?"

He gave me a sidelong smirk. "Just relax. We're almost there."

"Almost where?" I demanded, but he merely stared ahead in response.

We'd just rounded a sharp turn when Lloyd hit the brakes and pulled onto a gravel road. The Camry's undercarriage pinged and thwacked as we trundled down the weeded lane. When the car came to an abrupt halt, I took a look around.

No man's land.

No houses or outbuildings, no fences. Nothing but trees and brush. I'm not gonna lie; I felt a stab of fear, knowing this guy might well blow my brains out here. He could drag me into the underbrush and leave me to rot with no one the wiser.

Well, so be it, I decided. But I sure as hell wasn't about to make it easy for him.

To my consternation, he reached behind his back. I was half-way out the passenger door when his hand emerged. Not with a weapon, but a handkerchief.

"Settle down, Shane," he laughed. "I don't bite." He wiped his nose and snickered.

"Yeah, well I do."

"Noted." He opened his door and exited with a groan. "Damn sciatic nerve," he grumbled on his way to his feet. I leaned against the side of his car and waited for an explanation. I was pleasantly surprised when he got down to brass tacks without further prodding.

"Sorry to drag you out here, Shane. I can't risk no one seein' us together in town, and there ain't no tellin' if my car's bugged."

"You have reason to think it is?"

He frowned. "Let's just say I have reason to be cautious."

I nodded. "Fair enough. It was you who put that picture on my windshield, right? I mean, I've gotta have that part right."

"I was hopin' you'd use it to piece some things together. God knows no one else around these parts is brave enough to dare."

"Well, I'm sorry to report that I haven't put much together."

"Oh, I doubt that."

"What exactly were these guys into? I get Mr. Middleton, with his construction company and the dam. That much smells fishy as all hell, even if I don't know the particulars. And I know Alan Proctor was one cold-blooded son of a bitch. But I don't know a damn thing about Ralph Crowley, much less how he's connected to the others."

Lloyd glanced down the lane, which was pleasantly shaded. "I was a deputy sheriff for nearly twenty years, you know. Fifteen before Jim Thompson ever came along. I knew the second he walked in with a badge that I'd never get a crack at that sheriff star. Voters like to keep it in the family, you know?"

God, if all this bullshit boiled down to some stupid employee rivalry, I was going to be seriously pissed.

The old man must've read my mind because he waved his comment off as if it was irrelevant. "Don't get me wrong; I wasn't exactly tickled to death, but it wasn't that big of a deal. It was a callin' for me, my job. Sure, I had ambitions, but I wasn't in a big hurry. Bein' one of the good guys was enough for me."

"But you and Jim didn't get along?"

"I stomached Jim for as long as I could. He was competent enough, but he was what you might call 'ethically challenged.'"

He didn't have to tell me that.

"Anyway, in the end? It was that bastard Crowley who ruined my career." His expression turned bitter. "Ralph had a pretty bad drinkin' problem. He'd get hammered and jump behind the wheel without a second thought. I must've written him thirty citations one summer. They mysteriously disappeared from the books every time. Once, I even arrested the bastard."

I thought about the photo. Proctor, Crowley and Middleton had been chummy long before Lloyd came along. "I'm guessing that didn't go over well with Sheriff Proctor."

The old man guffawed. "That's puttin' it mildly. Told me if I ever arrested Ralph again, he'd have my badge."

I gave him an encouraging nod; now we were getting somewhere.

"Anyway, one afternoon I followed Crowley from a bar. It wasn't even dinner time and he was already plastered. I didn't have any plans to arrest him—I did value my job, just so you understand—so I just followed him. He drove through town and turned off for the dam." He shook his head, sucking in a whistling breath between teeth as round and gray as river rocks.

"The dam's awfully narrow," I pointed out. "It gets nerve-wracking enough when you're clean and sober."

"Exactly."

"So what happened?"

"Well, he managed to cross the dam with a few close calls, but then he gunned it at the end. Bastard hit a woman."

"You mean her car?"

"No, sir. I mean metal on bare skin. She'd been exploring below the dam and was crossing the road toward Yonker's. The impact damn near tore her in half."

"Holy shit…"

"So I intervened and did what any self-respecting deputy would do. I arrested his ass."

I cringed. "Uh-oh."

Spence nodded. "I called the local PD instead of the sheriff;

thought somethin' might stick if I could get 'em involved. But they hemmed and hawed once I told 'em who I had in custody. They didn't want any part of it."

"What about the GRDA? Did you reach out to them for help?"

The old man chuckled bitterly. "They put me on indefinite hold."

It made sense. While the Grand River Dam Authority was pretty hands-on these days, with officers patrolling land and water alike, they stuck to the water back then. The last thing they'd have wanted was to get mixed up in a bunch of controversy.

"What about witnesses?" I wanted to know. "Surely someone saw something."

"Far as I know, I'm it."

A grasshopper landed on my pantleg and then bounded away. "Wow," I breathed.

"She was stayin' at the campgrounds by the marina with her boyfriend. He came lookin' for her after the scene had been cleared. There were a few passersby, but we just waved 'em on."

"So what did you do?"

"I took a leap of faith and called Jim for help."

"Did he? Help, I mean?"

Lloyd's expression darkened. "He cut Crowley loose on the spot."

"What about the woman?"

"We collected her remains in a body bag and loaded her into the back of his patrol car." He chuckled humorlessly. "When I showed up for work the next day? Surprise, surprise. My desk was cleared out."

"Ouch."

"Yep."

From the trees, a rustling of foliage caught our attention. Lloyd paled noticeably. A moment later, a doe wandered into view. When she spotted us, she sniffed the air and dashed back into the woods in two graceful strides.

It took Lloyd a minute to recover. The poor guy must've been living in hell, all these years. Constantly looking over his shoulder, waiting for the other shoe to drop. It was no way to live.

I tried to get him back on track. "So, you got fired."

He nodded. "I tried to stay on top of the woman's death the best I could—I felt a personal responsibility, since I was the first responder—but not a word was ever muttered. No coroner's report on file, no obituary. Her boyfriend reported her missin' but, of course, she was never located."

He fished out his handkerchief and wiped his nose again, eyes darting uneasily to gaps in the tree line. "When Jim was finally elected, I considered blowin' the lid off the whole thing."

The thought made me dizzy. I couldn't help but imagine how different my life might've turned out without Jim Thompson behind a badge.

"Why didn't you?" I had to ask.

Lloyd shrugged. "My word against his. No body, no crime." He looked away abruptly, but not before I caught a glimpse of shame tugging at his cheeks. "He would've come after me, too," he added. "Not a doubt in my mind."

This was a lot to absorb. One detail in particular didn't make sense. "Crowley runs a used car lot. How does a guy that connected end up scraping by on chump change?"

"Oh, he was loaded, back in the day. He got a real kick out of flauntin' his lifestyle, spendin' money like it was an endless commodity. Then he developed a gamblin' problem. Blew through his entire fortune like that." Lloyd snapped his fingers for emphasis.

I'm not gonna lie; the story brought a smile to my face. "So what happened to the gang? Crowley and the sheriff don't exactly strike me as BFFs."

"Ray Middleton was the glue that kept the crew together. When Crowley went broke, Ray stepped up to help him. He came down with Alzheimer's four, maybe five years ago. It got to where Ray couldn't remember either one of them anymore. Jim and Ralph had a little fallin' out after that."

"Over what?" I wondered aloud.

Lloyd shrugged. "Hard to say."

I watched a honeybee disappear into the flute of a wildflower nearby. "Ray Middleton died a few days ago. Did you know?"

The former deputy sighed. "Yeah, I heard."

"He had a few visitors before he passed. One of them was the sheriff."

Lloyd shrugged noncommittally. "Not surprised. They were thick as thieves."

"Thing is, Middleton didn't get many visitors. No one had been to see him for a long while, from what I understand. Then a few guys show up out of the blue; next thing you know, he's dead."

"Could be a coincidence."

I nodded. "Could be. But what if Ray had an inkling his number was up?"

"You're thinkin' he wanted to clear his conscience?"

"Stranger things have happened."

Lloyd swatted a mosquito on his forearm. "Guess we'll never know."

"I gotta ask, Lloyd. What exactly did you hope to accomplish by involving me? I'm not a detective."

For a moment, Lloyd Spence looked as if he might bore a hole through me by the intensity of his gaze. He wasn't just appraising me, I thought; he was trying to invade my thoughts. Eventually, his eyes softened a bit and he smiled faintly. "Because out of everyone in this town, I figured you had the least to lose."

My cheeks flushed. "Forgive me if I'm less than flattered."

His expression sobered. "That picture, I knew it was the key to everything. And when I saw you at Mo's, I had this sense that as important as that picture was, you were even more important."

"Who took that picture, Lloyd? Was it you?"

A faint smile tugged at the corners of his mouth, but he shook his head. "Found it in Crowley's car the day of the accident. Not sure why I took it. Glad I did now, though."

In the distance, a siren came to life. Inexplicably, the shrill cry filled me with extraordinary dread. One look at Lloyd, and I knew he was feeling it, too.

"I think we'd better get back."

CHAPTER 24

July 14, 2018 ... 2:38 p.m.

I had no one to blame but myself for what happened next. After Lloyd drove me back to the liquor store and zipped off without another word, a police cruiser screamed by with lights flashing. Seconds later, another blew past just as I got my car started. My whole body tingled with trepidation as I pulled into traffic.

The cruisers raced to the highway and headed south. Following at a steady distance, I stuck with them all the way to Pryor Creek, twenty-seven miles away. The closer we got, the more panicked I became, because I knew deep down that something terrible was amiss. And that no matter how I cut it, I was to blame.

The cruisers screeched to a halt just outside the courthouse; four more vehicles—deputy sheriff and area PD cruisers alike—were parked haphazardly with lights strobing. I pulled into a parking space and sprinted inside.

I was too late, of course. There was nothing I or anyone else could do for Carl Whitehorse, now. He lay flat on his back in a pool of blood just outside the Mayes County Sheriff's office. Sheriff Thompson stood off to one side, shaking his head morosely. His eyes locked on mine for a moment and hardened.

My chest was heaving, my hands balling into iron fists.

"Whoa, buddy," a voice muttered over my shoulder. "Take it easy, now." A hand took me firmly by the arm and I instinctively wrenched it free, folding the fingers back just shy of breaking them.

"Goddamn it, Shane!"

I blinked in surprise. "Shit—sorry, David. I—I didn't mean to do that."

My friend shook his hand with a grimace. "You shouldn't be here," he hissed through clenched teeth.

"It's my fault," I replied.

David leaned in, eyes darting down the hall. "You better can that shit before someone hears you."

I glared at Sheriff Thompson, wanting for all I was worth to stomp his wrinkled ass into the marble floor.

"You hearing me, Shane? You need to leave. Now."

I took a calming breath. "Yeah, okay." I stole a parting glance over my shoulder; Sheriff Thompson gave me a pained glower and stomped into his office.

I followed David back to Langley in silence. My phone buzzed from the middle console at one point, but I didn't bother to answer.

Mo's was hardly a bustling venue in the best of times, but it was damn near empty today. David sat across from me and spooned sugar into his coffee. In a daze, I scarcely noticed Barbara's contemptuous glances from across the restaurant.

"You wanna tell me what the hell is going on?" David demanded.

I let my gaze swivel out the window as an ambulance lumbered down the road with its lights off.

"C'mon, Shane. Talk to me, man." His radio squawked from its perch on his shoulder; he twisted a knob to silence it.

I wanted to come clean. Honest to God, I wanted to unload the whole damn story right then and there. But I held back. The truth had already claimed one life today, and the day was still young.

Still, David was running out of patience. "What happened, Shane? What would possess Carl Whitehorse to march into that courthouse with a shotgun?"

I closed my eyes and shook my head. "Not here."

"Where, then?"

I swallowed hard, knowing that what I was about to do would change everything. For good or bad, it was simply too early to say.

"Let's take a ride," I said. "We need to make a stop first, though."

CHAPTER 25

July 14, 2018 ... 4:32 p.m.

David threw his cruiser into park and peered out the window where Fox Run ended at the water's edge. "What're we doing here, Shane?" A dollop of bird shit went *splat* on his windshield. "Dammit," he grumbled. "Just washed the car yesterday."

I unbuckled and opened the passenger door. As always, the water seemed to beckon me, and I was helpless but to heed its call. I trudged to the shallows, watching the lake swell and recede over the old concrete foundation. Had I really been down in there? Goosebumps streaked up my forearms.

David joined me at the water's edge with arms crossed. The restless whisper of blackbirds came from all directions.

"Just like that morning," I remarked. "All the damn birds."

With little forethought, I pried an old tree limb from the weeds nearby. "Used to be a house here," I pointed out. As if it wasn't already obvious. My hands shook as I plunged the branch into the water. It met concrete mere inches below the surface. I tried again, sidestepping a few feet over. Concrete again.

"What the hell is this, Shane?"

I swallowed and looked over my shoulder, catching his eye. I opened my mouth to speak, though I didn't have the slightest idea what to say. The stick dipped into the water again, but this time it met no resistance. I closed my eyes, praying to the god of shitty town justice that I was wrong. I desperately needed to be wrong. Yet when the stick snagged on something soft and buoyant, I knew I was right.

I gave the stick a shove and dragged it free. Bubbles gurgled to the surface. Curious, David crouched for a closer look. For a long moment, nothing happened. But then, as if in slow motion, a corpse rolled to the surface and wobbled with the waves. It was bloated beyond recognition with bits of flesh hanging off like fringe. A catfish wiggled from a hole in her torso and splashed a retreat back into the depths with a powerful tail.

David gasped and stumbled back. "Good Lord," he breathed.

I trained a somber gaze on him, my voice wavering. "I think there are more down there."

With eyes wild and cheeks pale, David's hand was on his holster now. "Jesus Christ, Shane. You better start talking, man."

"I will," I assured him. "But let's get the trail cam set up first."

Back at the car, I dumped a Benge Creek Outfitters bag and sifted through the contents on the passenger seat. I ripped into plastic packaging and spent a few minutes setting up the camera. Batteries.

An SD card. A Velcro strap. Satisfied, I attached it to a tree with a view of the water. Patterned in earth-toned camouflage, it all but disappeared against the vegetation when I stepped back.

David's jaw muscles flexed impatiently. "What the hell is that for?" he demanded.

"He'll be coming back. Probably tonight."

David hissed between his teeth. "Who are we talking about, Shane?"

My shoulders sagging, I shook my head. "You wouldn't believe me if I told you."

With his holster now unsnapped and a hand firmly gripping his sidearm, his eyes flashed angrily. "I suggest you try."

So, I told him.

The sun was creeping down the western horizon when David finally dropped me off at my car.

"What now?" I had to ask.

My friend shook his head, hands strangling the steering wheel. "I'm not sure yet," he replied. "Let's just concentrate on getting through the night, for now."

I felt the blood drain from my face. Jesus... I'd forgotten all about tonight. This was it—the twenty-fifth anniversary of the drowning was upon us.

"Go someplace safe and lock yourself in for the night, you hear?"

With a nod, I stood by my car and tried to keep it together.

"Whatever happens, David, I just wanna say…" I hesitated. What exactly did I want to say? A thousand memories seemed to flicker by, most all but forgotten. Too many to count, yet in each, this guy had been there for me. Building me up while most of the town tried to tear me down. "Thanks. For being my friend."

He nodded almost imperceptibly. "Right back at you, buddy."

I slumped into my rental as David took off. "I'm so sorry, Carl," I whispered. God, if only I'd kept my damn mouth shut. If only I had let sleeping dogs lie, Carl Whitehorse would still be alive.

If only, if only. I was so tired of those. Tired of it all.

My phone pulsed and I answered in a daze.

"Shane! Finally caught you."

I groaned inwardly. "Hey, Devon."

"How's it going, buddy?"

Buddy. Devon and I had never been anything approaching buddies.

"I've been better," I said, "but I'll be okay."

"And your mom?" I could hear him tapping an impatient finger on the outer shell of his phone.

"She passed."

He hissed appropriately. "Ah, shit. I'm sorry to hear that, man."

"It wasn't a shock or anything," I reminded him. "We knew it was coming. It's why I took time off."

Devon hesitated, not sure where to go from there. "Listen," he finally said. "I know I told you to take all the time you need, but things are getting a little backed up here. I've got you on the schedule for Monday. Can I count on you to be here?"

I cringed. "Nah, man. I'm really sorry, but there's just too much going on right now to head back that soon."

Devon was quiet for a second. "Okay. How about Tuesday?"

I kneaded my temples. "Devon, to be honest, this really isn't a good time to talk. Maybe I can call you—"

Devon cut me off. "I'm sorry, Shane. Really. But you know how it is, man."

I smiled bitterly. "I get it. The orders never stop."

"Exactly. I'm calling you from home on a Saturday, man. You think I don't have better things to do?" His irritation was understandable, but it still annoyed the hell out of me. "Tell you what," he said, his tone back under control. "Call me in the morning and let's see if we can come up with a game plan."

"Thanks, Devon. I really appreciate it."

"Okay, then. We'll talk soon, my man."

If I'd known how crazy things were about to get, I'd have saved us both the trouble and quit.

July 14, 2018 … 8:07 p.m.

Winnie called just after eight o'clock. Mindy and I were nursing a sugar coma on the couch, thanks to a dinner of Lo Mein noodles and chocolate chip cookies. I almost didn't answer it. I only bothered because Winnie wasn't one for idle chat; if she was calling, something was up.

Groaning with the effort, I managed to slap the phone to my

ear. "Hey," I muttered.

"Wherever you are, you best stay put tonight."

"That's the plan. Mindy's heading out to help guard the shore, but I'm staying here."

"Good, because you're liable to get lynched, otherwise."

I frowned. "Did some of my pals stop by?"

"Showed up in five vehicles. They pounded on the door for a while and then took off."

"Surprised you didn't answer with a shotgun."

"If I'd been in there, I might have."

My brow furrowed. "You still haven't moved into the house?"

Winnie was silent for a second. "Ah, hell, Shane. It's just…" A tremulous sigh. "It's just too soon."

"Okay."

"Anyway, stay put, would you?"

"Will do," I promised, though I had no intention of laying low at Mindy's anymore. If the townsfolk were actively looking for me, it wouldn't be long before they tracked me here. I figured we had fifteen minutes—just enough time to button the place up and make ourselves scarce for the night.

I was wrong.

A pounding on Mindy's front door announced the arrival of Langley's wannabe enforcers less than five minutes later. Not that any formal announcement was necessary, considering five pairs of headlights blared through the windows, accompanied by the honking of horns and slamming of doors.

"Come on out, Ghost Boy," a voice barked from the stoop. "We know you're in there."

Mindy appeared in the bedroom doorway with a hairbrush in hand. Her expression turned fearful. "Oh, shit..."

Another voice joined in. "You're gonna pay for what you did to my truck, asshole!"

Ah, good old Jackson. Glad to know I scored a point; I'd be shocked if he ever got that smell out of his upholstery.

A thought struck, and I had to ask—even if I'd already intuited the answer. "Where does your roommate work?" I asked Mindy.

"Jack's Plumbing. She's a receptionist. Why?"

I closed my eyes and nodded. "Well, shit. Guess I should've seen that coming."

"You don't think she..." Her eyes flashed to the front door and back, her mouth gaping in betrayal. "That bitch!"

With a shrug of resignation, I ambled to the door, peeking out the window along the way. Silhouettes of varying heights and builds resolved against the headlights.

Mindy dropped the bag and rushed to my side. "No, Shane—they'll kill you."

"I'll be fine," I lied.

I suppose I'd known all along that it would come down to this. I'd been fighting for redemption most of my life, after all—with fists, with a sharp tongue. Despite the intensity with which my hometown loathed me, I had them beat hands down. No one could despise me more than I despised myself. Tonight was as good a night as any to die.

Mindy must've read some of this in my eyes, because she lunged past me to block the door.

"C'mon, Mindy!" a voice called out. "Send your little friend out to play!"

I reached around her to turn the doorknob, but Mindy leaned back against the door. I tried to move her aside and she resisted. I could've pushed harder—plenty hard enough to get the job done—but I didn't want to hurt her. She needed to make her own peace with what was about to happen.

The knob wobbled in my hand as someone tried to open the door from outside. "Get your ass out here, freak! Last time we're asking."

"Mindy?" I said softly.

She looked at me with terror in her eyes, breathing wildly between bared teeth. She didn't reply; instead, she leaned harder against the door.

"Mindy?" I tried again. "If I don't go out, they're coming in."

She blinked, shook her head.

"You don't want a bunch of crazed men terrorizing your living space, do you?"

"I won't let them in."

As if to prove her wrong, the door heaved open from the outside. Shoving Mindy aside, I threw my weight against the door and heaved it closed again.

"I'm coming out," I snapped. "Just give me a second."

"Please don't, Shane."

I wiped a tear from her cheek. "I'm sorry, Mindy. This is the way it has to be. I love you."

Before she could frame a reply, I opened the door and plunged outside.

CHAPTER 26

July 14, 1968 ... 1:35 p.m.

I was plodding along the road, sweating profusely. It was a long walk and I was hot and tired, but I had to keep going.

A vehicle passed me and then hit the brakes; it backed up until I was looking in the front passenger window.

"Hot day to be footin' it to town," came a voice from within.

"I'll be okay," I replied with a forced smile. I wiped the sweat from my upper lip with the back of my hand.

"How 'bout a ride?"

I stole a glance into the vehicle; it was a big one with a shiny chrome bumper. I spied two men in front, two more in the back. There was no room for me in there; these men were up to no good. Shaking my head, I kept walking.

The driver exited the car and rounded the long hood, smiling.

"Now, hold on there, young lady," he chuckled. He gave me a wink as if I wasn't old enough to be his grandmother. "Are you new in town? Thought I knew everyone, but I don't recognize you."

I shook my head again and tried to move on.

The man blocked my path. Tall with stork-like legs, he wore a vest with a metal star pinned to the chest. "Tell you what," he said with a toothy smile. "No hard feelings if you don't wanna ride, but can you do me a small favor?" He smiled genially.

Outside my field of view, the mechanical sounds of doors opening and closing crept in.

A different man—this one short and stout with a funny hat—approached with something in his hands. Something black and unfamiliar. A white man's invention.

"This here's my new toy," the man explained. "It's a Polaroid camera. Takes instant pictures."

My gaze darted to the lawman—the other two passengers of the vehicle had settled beside him—and back to the camera.

"All you gotta do is point it and push this button," the short one explained in a voice that was too soothing, and therefore patronizing.

"Please, I need to go," I muttered.

"Sure, sure. Just, if you wouldn't mind, would you take our picture first? Won't take but a second."

I didn't know how to take a picture, and I wasn't in the mood to learn. My arthritic knees were swelling by the minute, so I shook my head.

The lawman chimed in. "It's about as easy as it gets, little lady. Here, let the kid show you how."

The boy glanced at the lawman with uncertainty.

"Go on, son. Get to it."

The boy fetched the camera as the men crowded together. As he approached, he kept his gaze trained down. I tried to ignore the tremble in his hands, though it was impossible to overlook.

Just do what the white men say, I told myself. *Do it and they'll leave you alone.*

Still, the boy was nervous. And in my experience, white boys didn't get nervous easily.

I let the boy demonstrate holding the device to his eye; he pretended to push the button, making a clicking noise with his tongue.

"See?" he remarked. "It's easy."

He handed the contraption to me and I accepted it with reluctance. I held it to my eye and framed the men through the glass. They cinched tighter together and smiled. When I pushed the button, the invention made a clicking sound.

I didn't see the blow coming.

It struck the back of my head, knocking me senseless. Suddenly, the ground was rushing up at me, and I was helpless to stop it. I closed my eyes. When I opened them seconds later, someone was dragging me into the woods by my hair, laughing. He let me fall to the ground in a small clearing, surrounded by trees. I tried to stand, but the tall man pushed me down with his boot.

"Hold her for me, Ray," he said, loosening his belt.

The short man grinned and leveraged my head against the ground by my necklace. It frightened me, at first—not being able to breathe—but soon enough, I'd wish for him to pull the leather as hard as he could.

July 14, 2018 ... 9:21 p.m.

I had no concept for the passage of time when I opened my eyes. My mind spun, trying to process the dream despite waking to unfamiliar surroundings. With my hands cuffed behind me, my ribs screamed in agony. I was alone in a jail cell, splayed down the length of a concrete bench. The miasma of dried piss and vomit hung thick in the air. I sat up, grimacing. My head throbbed.

Abruptly, the sheriff appeared beyond the bars. "Good. You're awake."

"What the hell am I doing here?" I demanded.

"You just don't know when to quit, do you?" was his curt reply. "I warned you to clear out."

"That you did."

"You're lucky I showed up when I did. Barely got a scratch on ya."

"My hero."

"Nah, Mindy's your hero, Shane. If she hadn't called me, you'd be in a body bag. Those boys were primed to rip you apart."

Deputy Mullen stepped into view. "Why, hello there, Sleeping Beauty," he snickered, slapping a Maglite against his palm. "How's the head?"

Sheriff Thompson rolled his eyes. "Cool it, Chad."

"Am I under arrest?" I asked.

The sheriff smirked. "Yep."

"What for?"

He folded his arms across a barrel chest. "Oh, assault. Disturbin' the peace. Possession. Maybe fraud." He flashed a set of coffee-stained dentures. "Don't you worry—we'll come up with sumthin."

"I want my phone call."

Chad tapped the bars with his flashlight. "Hey, smartass—you're not exactly in a position to be makin' demands, are ya?"

Anger welled up within me, buoying me to my feet. "It's all about to come out, Sheriff. You can't cover it up anymore, and you sure as hell can't outrun it. You realize that, don't you?"

Chad blew an amused raspberry, but Sheriff Thompson? His smile twitched.

"All these years, and no one suspected you," I muttered. "Not the town, not even your asshole deputy." Maybe he hadn't pulled the trigger in my dreams, but it was clear that he'd worked through his reservations over time.

Deputy Mullen sneered. "Suspected him of... what the hell's he talkin' about, boss?"

"How many have there been, Sheriff? Five? Ten?"

The sheriff's face went blank—placid, even. "Chad, would you give us the room, please?"

The deputy stole a sidelong glance at his boss. He looked like he wanted to say something; perhaps wisely, he stalked off without another word.

I plopped back onto the bench and leaned against the painted cinderblock wall. Sheriff Thompson eyed me for several seconds, uncertainty gleaming in his baggy eyes. He stuffed a plug of Skoal into his mouth and spat into an empty Pepsi bottle.

"Just what the hell are you goin' on about?" he demanded, his voice hushed.

"You're a cold-blooded murderer."

He sighed and leaned against the bars. "You're wrong, Gibson. I've never killed a soul." His eyes sandwiched shut for a second. He took a weary breath. "Not until Carl, that is. And it ain't like he left me much choice. Can't imagine what he was thinkin'."

"I'm supposed to believe that? What, you just let your stepdaddy do all the dirty work for you?"

His eyes widened. We both knew what I was talking about, even if he couldn't bring himself to acknowledge it. I could understand his hesitation, though. It shouldn't be possible for me to know, after all; Middleton was dead, and Crowley would sooner eat dirt than give me the time of day.

"I don't know what you're talkin' about," he snapped, a bloom of color burgeoning on his wrinkled cheeks.

"I'll bet you think about it all the time, don't you? The old Indian woman. Does it turn you on? Get you good and riled up to do it again? We both know there have been others." Lowering my voice and cupping my mouth secretively, I added, "I know where the bodies are."

The corners of Thompson's eyes crinkled in disbelief; abruptly, they went cold.

"It's over," I said softly. "Throw your weight around all you want, but you're going down."

He glared openly. "Not gonna happen, Gibson." Slowly, his mouth stretched into a wide grin. "We'll see who's goin' down soon enough." He turned a dial on his shoulder radio and mumbled into the mic. "Anything to report yet?"

The radio crackled to life. "Nuthin yet, boss. Winnifred's here, though. Throwin' a proper fit."

Jim turned a Cheshire grin on me. "She gives you any more trouble, arrest her ass."

"Will do," squawked the radio.

My cheeks flushed. "What the hell are you guys doing at my mom's place?"

He shrugged, beaming with satisfaction. "I warned you to leave town," he chuckled. "This is on you."

At once, it hit me. The cigar box. They were looking for his box of trophies. Which meant the sheriff had known his ex planted it. Actually, now that I thought about it, he'd probably been the mastermind all along. Why hadn't I seen it before?

I considered keeping all this to myself, but I couldn't think of any downside to sharing it now. Whereas it *did* have a considerable upside; I'd get to watch his shit-eating grin crumble. "You after that little trophy box Alice brought over?" I asked innocently.

Sure enough, his grin slipped; his eyes widened. Totally worth it.

"Yeah, it's long gone, Sheriff. You're wasting your time."

With a defeated frown, he crossed his arms. "Goddammit, I want you to leave Mindy alone, Shane. You don't understand what you're dealin' with."

I laughed bitterly. "God, you're arrogant. Nobody's good enough for her, is that it? You'd honestly rather she wither up and die an old maid than settle down with someone who doesn't meet your standards."

Thompson smiled with jaded amusement. "Is that what you think?"

"By all means, correct me if I'm wrong."

He chuckled humorlessly. "You don't have any goddamn idea what's really goin' on, do you, kid?"

"I know you're a murdering piece of shit. What else is there to know?"

The sheriff sighed between the hollows of his teeth. "I never liked you, Gibson, but I never pegged you for an idiot until now. My mistake."

"What the hell is that supposed to mean?"

Thompson stabbed the air in my direction with a beefy finger. "I've tried to protect Mindy—and you, for that matter—but she's beyond help. Ain't no happily ever after with that girl. Not for you, not for nobody."

"Not if you have anything to say about it."

Sheriff Thompson closed his eyes and licked his lips. "I think we're done here," he muttered. With that, he left me alone to stew.

I managed to sleep for a while, despite the discomforts of handcuffs and a concrete bed, but whatever sleep I managed to get wasn't restful. Eventually, I gave up the fight and sat up to stretch my back.

Over and over, I replayed my conversation with the sheriff in my head. I'd be lying if I said it wasn't at least mildly satisfying, getting to confront him like that. But the longer I considered his responses, the more certain I became that something was off. I was missing something.

My thoughts drifted back to the drowning, poking and prodding the memory for some small detail buried within.

Maybe she was pointin' at someone else, Carl Whitehorse had suggested, regarding the Lady of the Water. There had been something behind me, I recalled. A shuffling in the grass. Probably a squirrel or something, but what if—

"Hey."

The voice startled me. With an annoyed glance, I spat, "Run along, Skidmark."

Chad's expression darkened and he opened his mouth to fire off a retort. Only, words failed him. He swallowed and took a step toward the bars. "It's just us. I'm gonna let you out, but you gotta hurry."

"What the hell are you talking about, Chad? Hurry with what?"

The deputy rubbed the bridge of his nose. "Don't be dense, Shane. The evidence room is down the hall. Last door on your right."

It clicked then, what this was all about. I rose and approached the bars. "So you're working for Biggun?"

Chad rolled his eyes and unlocked the cell door. "I don't work for Biggun. I just help him out once in a while."

"Mm-hmm."

"Just get out here, asshole."

Grudgingly, I complied. "What am I after, exactly?"

"E27."

"Uh, say again?"

"Aisle E, bay 27." Chad spun me around to unlock my cuffs.

"You'll find a box there. Grab it and walk it straight outside."

"What if someone tries to stop me?"

The deputy shrugged. "Who's gonna stop you? It's almost four in the mornin', and every badge within fifty miles is off guardin' the lake."

"Except you."

He shrugged. "All in due time."

A moment later, I was tiptoeing down the marble hallway to the evidence room. A wave of panic surged through me when the doorknob wouldn't turn. "Shit!" I hissed. "It's locked!"

From the end of the hall, watching with amusement, Chad popped a stick of chewing gum into his mouth. "Ain't locked. It just sticks. Put some muscle into it, little lady."

I torqued the knob harder and, sure enough, it broke free. Inside, the evidence room was small and jam-packed. Cluttered shelves divided the space into dim corridors, each labeled with a letter. Despite the impression of disarray, the room was surprisingly organized. It took less than thirty seconds to find aisle E, another minute to find bay 27. The box stored there was sealed tight with a band of red tape. I dragged it off the shelf and strode swiftly back into the hallway.

Outside, Chad had pulled up to the door and was waiting in the driver's seat. Seeing me, he waved me onward.

CHAPTER 27

July 14, 2018 … 10:35 p.m.

The old Buick smelled like cigars and Bengay.

"Couldn't have borrowed something a little more age-appropriate, huh?"

"It's what I could find. Ain't got much of a motor pool at the moment. Still beats that piece of shit you've been drivin' around town."

For once, I had to agree with Chad.

The deputy drove a mile under the speed limit all the way back to Langley. He didn't say much, and I wasn't feeling particularly chatty either. On the other hand, I had to wonder what was in store for me. It made sense to let me do the dirty work of plundering the evidence room—my iniquity was undoubtedly immortalized on camera, after all—but why keep me around now?

Kick me loose or lock me up again—it wouldn't have been hard for Chad to sell either scenario. But to bring me along? I couldn't think of a single explanation that gave me anything but a pit in my stomach.

Soon after we got into town, Chad turned off for the dam.

"So where are we headed?" I dared to ask.

"Biggun's got a guy waitin' by Yonker's. You're gonna make the drop."

"You're kidding, right? At Yonker's—tonight of all nights?" I blew a raspberry. "You and Biggun need to quit sampling your own product."

"It'll be good and crowded. Easy to get lost in the bustle."

I shrugged, at a loss. "Okay, fine. And then what?"

Chad chewed his lip thoughtfully as we reached the dam. "Haven't decided yet. Might just shoot you." Despite his smile of amusement, I suspected he was at least half serious.

The road in and out of the marina was lined with parked cars. "Looks like the whole damn county showed up," Chad remarked with a whistle.

"Just to be clear, you want me to make a drop in full view of all these people?"

The deputy grinned. "Yep."

Shit. This couldn't possibly end well. I'd be committing a felony surrounded by witnesses—people who would be quick to recognize me. Especially tonight of all nights. Before I could put together an exit strategy, the car slowed to a stop near an RV.

"Make it quick," Chad said, glancing at his watch.

Scowling, I opened the car door and toted the box to the RV.

The door creaked open a second before I reached it.

"Special delivery," I muttered.

A pair of meaty hands relieved me of the box and slammed the door.

"You're welcome," I grumbled and headed back toward the car. It was then that I noticed just how crowded the marina was. Darkened silhouettes slipped in and out of focus in all directions. Chad was right—I needn't have worried about being noticed; it was far too crowded, too chaotic.

Would she really reappear tonight—the Lady of the Water? Would more children die?

Not if I had anything to say about it.

Chad was motioning me back into the car, but I'd made up my mind. Before he could so much as unbuckle, I barreled down the lane toward the boat ramp. I heard the car door open and shut behind me, but I wasn't worried. Chad wasn't the brightest bulb on the tree, but even he was too smart to open fire with all these people around.

The shore was crowded for several hundred yards, I realized, the beams of countless flashlights stabbing the air thoroughly. The euphoria of relief brought a smile of satisfaction to my face. No one was getting past these people.

"Get your ass back here, Gibson!" Chad called after me. The sound of him crashing through bushes and underbrush assured me that he wasn't gaining on me. With any luck, I'd disappear into the crowd before—

Suddenly, I saw her… the Lady of the Water.

She glowed like a celestial body on the far side of the lake. My heart lurched at the sight of her, at the implications of where she was. There were no flashlights sweeping the shore over there, no able-bodied volunteers gathered to protect would-be victims. Could they really not see her?

I was running for the water even before I realized it. I surged past a cluster of volunteers in orange vests, who shouted in surprise. One made a grab for my arm but stopped short once he recognized me. "Let him go," he growled. "It's the damn Ghost Boy. Good riddance."

There were some halfhearted protests, but I was past the shallows by then. My shoes filled with water and weighed me down like bricks, so I kicked them off and plowed into the depths, my gaze never wavering from the woman in the distance.

This part of the lake wasn't wide, thankfully, but for a man nursing a rib injury, it was an ocean. Overhead, blackbirds flittered by in the darkness, squawking like hungry gulls and plunging into the water.

My side screamed in agony, but I lassoed the pain, letting it spur me on. I was halfway across when the first cramp hit. It seized my thigh, rendering the leg useless. Grimacing, I flipped onto my back and floated, propelling myself onward by scissoring cupped hands at my sides. Birds slapped the water around me now like hailstones. Yet above their racket, a more substantial splash sounded from the looming shore as someone sloshed into the water. Leg be damned, I flipped back over and gave it everything I had left. The woman was a stone's throw away now, beckoning darkened figures into her deadly midst.

I surged past her and caught a handful of t-shirt, dragging a little boy onto the rocky shallows. He coughed and plopped to his knees on dry ground. A splash behind me announced another victim, this one thrashing like a whale.

"Stop!" I screamed, though I honestly wasn't sure who I was screaming at—the children or the woman. Nevertheless, I dove into the churning water and speared toward the disturbance.

To my surprise, this one was a man—an old timer I recognized with the rude abruptness of a flick to the ear.

Ralph Crowley.

He went limp when I grabbed his arm, yet when I tried to steer him back to safety, he fought free of my grip and lunged toward deeper water in determined strides.

"Please, stop!" I cried again, this time to the woman.

Her beauty was transfixing, I couldn't help but notice, but it was different now than when I was a kid—less overwhelming, for one. Perhaps because she wasn't calling me in? It was hard to say. I swam in her direction with what little gas I had left in the tank. I passed Crowley just as his head dipped beneath the surface. I snatched at the water in a last-ditch effort to save him, but it was no use. The old man was gone.

A searing pain shot up my wrist.

At once, a hand was on my chest, long, spindly fingers holding me at bay. When I looked up, gazing into eyes that glistened like the lake itself, the Lady of the Water shook her head gently. Behind me, the telltale splash of another victim broke the silence. "Please," I cried, tears boiling from my eyes. "Please, stop! Take me instead."

Even as I spoke the words, I realized how cowardly they were. A bystander might easily have mistaken them for something heroic, but they were a manifestation of self-loathing and nothing more. I wasn't merely resigned to die; I wanted it more than anything in the world. It was as if my entire miserable life had funneled into the singular promise of that moment.

I could be free of it all.

The woman smiled sadly, as if she sensed my desperation. Her lips remained still, yet at once I could hear her familiar song, lulling me to comfort, to blessed sleep. The edge of my consciousness closed in, and—

CHAPTER 28

July 15, 2018 … 6:35 a.m.

The irksome beeps of hospital gadgetry dragged me from the soft bosom of deep sleep. I was tucked into a hospital bed with an IV trailing from the back of one hand. In a nearby corner, David—unshaven and out of uniform—was scrolling up the screen of his iPhone. I tried to sit up, wincing at a crick in my neck.

David shot to his feet. "Hey, don't try to move around, Shane. Just take it easy."

"What happened?" I croaked. "I thought…" I should've been dead.

David patted me on the shin. "Well, you damn near drowned, for one. And then there's the snakebite."

"The what?"

"Cottonmouth. He was probably after one of those birds, but

he got you good."

I allowed my gaze to travel down my arms, one of which was encased in bandages and a cold pack.

"They started the antivenom already, so just relax. It's gonna be fine."

"Did anyone—" I tried to ask, but my nerves choked the words off.

"Just one."

My stomach clenched like a fist. "Shit. A kid?"

David shook his head. "No kids." He swallowed and a tremor traveled across his face. "We found thirty-five kids asleep by the water," he said. A tear went rogue down one cheek and he caught it with the palm of his hand. "Damnedest thing. Whatever was about to happen, it just…" He shook his head and shrugged, his eyes squeezing shut. "It stopped. I think…" His eyes sprang open again. "I think you stopped it, Shane. Somehow."

My own tears were flowing now. I closed my eyes and sighed with relief, imagining I could hear the entire town sigh with me. "Thank God."

A weary nod of confirmation. "Except for old man Crowley. He owns that used car lot over by—"

"I know who he is."

My old friend nodded and took a deep breath. He cleared his throat. "Listen, I checked the trail cam a while ago." His mouth tightened as he framed his words.

I stiffened, waiting for the verdict.

"We got clean footage of Sheriff Thompson dragging five bodies from the basement of that flooded house and loading them into his Tahoe."

I released my breath, only just now aware that I'd been holding it at all. "Where'd he take them?"

"We're working on that." David's hands clasped across his beltline. "Listen, there's something else, Shane. It's Mindy. She's, uh… she's down the hall."

"Can you send her in?"

David's face twitched. "She's not here to visit, Shane."

In my medicated stupor, I could only stare dumbly in response.

"She was admitted shortly after you were."

The room began to spin as my pulse picked up its pace. One of the nearby machines beeped in warning. "Oh, God. What happened? Is she okay?"

"She was on one of the volunteer teams guarding the shoreline. Apparently, she wandered into the water this morning. She was out quite a ways before anyone noticed."

My whole body was trembling now. "No…"

David held up his hands to ward off any hasty conclusions. "She's okay, buddy. The paramedics were able to revive her."

I must've looked like death itself, because David stepped closer to loom over me, resting a hand on my shoulder.

"She's in stable condition, okay? Everything's gonna be fine."

"Probably should've led with that," I muttered.

It was a lot to absorb, but not enough to fill in all the blanks. How had I gotten here, for example? The last thing I remembered was sliding under water. And how long had Mindy been in the water? Had she sustained any brain damage?

I was about to ask these questions and more, but before I could summon the words, a deep wail gusted through the room like a stormy wind.

"Shane!"

Winnie barreled into the room with tears streaking down splotchy cheeks. "Oh, thank you, Jesus," she sobbed and lunged to my bedside, where she damn near strangled me in a bear hug.

CHAPTER 29

I wish I could say that Sheriff Thompson got what he deserved, but he was still breathing. Even if it was from a jail cell. There would be a trial soon. The DA had agreed to forgo the death penalty if Thompson would divulge the whereabouts of the bodies. They were recovered in a thickly wooded stretch of land outside city limits. He'd wrapped them in plastic tarps and buried them in a shallow grave.

Days later, Alice Thompson stepped forward to unburden her soul. With her help, two more bodies were recovered less than a hundred yards from her house, buried under a thick patch of overgrowth.

I'm not gonna lie—it was hard to stomach how much she'd known all along.

There was no holding the media at bay, once word got out. They swarmed the town like a biblical plague of locusts. I stayed with Mindy for a few nights, pitching every argument I could muster to persuade her to leave with me. The harder I tried, the more resolute she became.

Still reeling over the drowning anniversary—not necessarily the death of Crowley, who wasn't well-liked, and not to mention the horror of Sheriff Thompson's iniquities—the town seemed more vulnerable than ever. Stores closed at odd hours, people barricaded themselves indoors. Likewise, Mindy was understandably distant after the anniversary. Hell, so was I.

Winnie drove me to Tulsa, where I returned my rental car and paid an arm and a leg. Plus a toe for good measure, thanks to the flat tire and scratch down one side. No matter. The insurance settlement had finally come through, and I'd be reimbursed for most of my rental costs. I'd buy another car soon enough. Nothing fancy like the Mustang; just something cheap and dependable. In the meantime, I didn't mind walking.

I lost my job, which was no surprise. Funny how little it bothered me. I felt a little guilty for leaving Devon in a bind, but other than that? Nada.

With a little help from my friend Adam, I managed to get out from under my lease back in St. Louis. My belongings were auctioned off, but I didn't care. I sent him a copy of the video, by the way—starring Chad and his flashlight. The Mayes County Sheriff's Department cut him loose days later. Adam wanted to file a suit against the department on my behalf, but I didn't want any part of that. It was enough for me to know that Skidmark Mullen wouldn't be abusing a badge anymore.

August 22, 2018 … 11:25 a.m.

Biggun reached out once more. One of his muscleheads plucked me right off the shoulder of the road like I was a half-eaten bag of microwave popcorn and drove me out to the abandoned barbeque joint.

"Heard my boy Chad's out of the game," Biggun said with deadpan eyes as I walked in. "Damn shame, too. Ain't gonna be easy to replace him."

Well, shit. I guess for every yin, there's gotta be a yang; this was an angle I hadn't considered before sending that video off to Adam.

So be it. I stiffened for the beating I knew had to be coming.

Biggun sighed. "Relax, my man," he said. "I'm gonna let it slide."

My eyes must've bugged, because Biggun laughed long and hard. At once, his expression softened. "That little boy you pulled from the water? He's my nephew."

The room seemed to spin a little. "How do you know about that?" I had to ask. There had been no witnesses to speak of. Or… had there?

"He told me. Said you brought him back to shore and told the lady to take you instead."

My heart crawled into the back of my throat. "He… he saw the woman?"

Biggun shook his head. "Honestly, I got no idea what he actually saw, but it don't matter. Point is, he says you saved his life, man."

Biggun tried to give me money, even a car—free and clear—but I demurred.

"There's gotta be sumthin I can do, man," he insisted. "That kid, I love him like my own son. If you hadn't been there…" He shook a head that would put an oversized watermelon to shame. "Goddamn, I don't even wanna think about it."

"Does this mean we're square?" I dared to ask.

"Yeah. We're square."

"And your guys won't sell to Mindy anymore?"

The man's eyes narrowed a little, but he kept his cool and nodded. "You got my word, man." He took a moment to eye his boys individually. "Y'all hear that? The Thompson girl's off limits. If she comes to you, you ain't got nuthin to sell. We clear?"

I felt the weight of a giant slip off my shoulders, hearing those words.

"You wanna toke?" the man asked, offering me a glass pipe. "On the house. The least I can do."

"Nah, I'm good, Biggun. Could use a ride back into town, though. I was on my way to the store when… you know."

Biggun waved this off. "Say no more." He put the pipe to his lips and fired up a green Bic lighter. When he was done, he passed it off to one of his buddies. "Yo, Slip," he said, coughing to clear the chemical residue from his throat. "Take my friend here to the store and buy him any damn thing he wants."

I stole a glance over my shoulder at Slip. His eyebrows shot up. "For real?"

Biggun frowned. "Did I stutter?"

August 23, 2018 … 7:14 p.m.

Mindy could've been anything she wanted, if only she'd found a way to put that town behind her. I couldn't begin to fathom what kept her there on such a formidable leash, and I doubted I ever would. It was time to make peace with that.

"You know I hate this town," I told her with a wan smile. We were cuddled up on her couch, watching Friends reruns on Netflix.

Her gaze dropped to her lap. "I know you do."

"And I think we can agree this town hates me back."

A faint smile embellished her perfect lips. "Oh, I don't know about that; I think they might be comin' around."

"How's that?"

Mindy plucked a lent ball off my shirt and shrugged. "When was the last time anyone refused you service or even threatened to beat your ass?"

She had a point there. I slipped off the couch and took her hand; she swallowed hard, looking up at me with wet doe eyes.

"You're leaving, aren't you?" she whispered.

"That depends."

Her eyes went half-lidded with uncertainty.

I reached into my pants pocket and produced a ring. Set in white gold, the diamond was modest but beautiful. I didn't have a job or even a home anymore, and I didn't give a damn at the moment. The only thing that had ever made me feel whole was right here in front of me. Maybe it was a sickness, my love for Mindy. Maybe I truly was obsessed, as Barbara had so eloquently put it when I first strolled back into town. The truth was that it didn't matter much anymore.

Mindy gaped at the ring, at me.

I dropped to one knee beside the couch—just as I'd practiced in my head a hundred times. "I love you, Mindy Thompson. More than I hate this town; even more than it hates me."

She blinked.

"Thing is, I don't need the town to love me. Just you. You're the only thing I've ever been sure about. I've loved you since that first kiss on the dock, and I always will."

Mindy laughed and wiped her eyes. She kissed me then, long and hard. I swear, a lifetime of sorrow gave up on me in that moment. I felt it depart like a mob of disgruntled spirits, and in its absence rose a sense of peace I hadn't experienced since I was a kid.

She leaned forward and drew me onto the couch next to her, wrapping me in her arms. She pulled my shirt off and kissed my neck, running fingernails up and down my back. She was wearing a skirt, which accentuated her long, toned legs. My hands glided up her thighs, disappearing beneath the fabric. She wasn't wearing any panties. I was already hard, but that took me from stone to iron.

And that wasn't the only thing that was different.

"God," I groaned blissfully, letting my fingers explore her freshly shaven pussy. It might've been the sexiest thing I'd ever felt. I wouldn't have thought it possible to get any harder, yet I did. "Me likey," I managed to croak.

"Thought you might," she breathed, her hips grinding against my fingers.

"I should probably get a closer look." My breath hitched as she stroked me over my jeans.

"Maybe later," she panted, and went to work on my zipper. She crawled on top of me and guided me inside her even as I liberated her of her shirt and bra. God, she felt so good. She leaned into me and rocked slowly at first, picking up speed when I lifted my head to kiss her nipples. She breathed in tiny moans that grew louder, more urgent with each movement.

Mindy got there first, but only just. This wasn't necessarily a product of my superior handiwork, though I'd love to take the credit. She came quickly. Always had. And just as always, the feel of her climaxing with me inside her—her lithe body clenching on my throbbing cock—only hastened me closer to finishing. I didn't want to finish yet, though. I wanted this moment to last forever. I wanted to spend an eternity looking into those eyes, hearing her breath against my neck.

But I couldn't hold it any longer.

Sensing this, Mindy kissed me deeply, her breasts heaving against my bare shoulders. At once, the world exploded with sweet release.

She collapsed on top of me and nuzzled against my neck. "God, I love you, Shane."

The words stunned me. "You've never told me that before."

It was true. As much as I'd longed to hear those very words, Mindy had never once uttered them in my presence.

"I know," she said in a whisper. "I'm sorry for that. But they aren't just words for me. I don't take them lightly. I needed to be sure first."

"And you're sure now?"

She propped onto her elbows and gazed into my eyes. "I've never been more certain of anything in my life."

My heart pounded like a heavy bag. Tears stung my eyes and I managed to stop them before making a weeny of myself.

"So…" I said, clearing the emotion from my throat. "Is that a yes, then?"

Mindy poked me in the stomach. "Yes, you dummy," she giggled. Then her features softened. "Yes. I'll marry you."

God, if only the story ended there. If I could go back in time, I'd snip it clean and die a happy man.

If only, if only.

CHAPTER 30

The dreams had stopped after the anniversary. Yet months later, completely out of the blue? Here I was again, trapped in someone else's tragic memory. Worse, it was eerily familiar.

Some fifty feet from shore, a low moaning came from the woods. I froze and listened intently. Soon enough, it sounded again, this time with a higher pitch. I plodded carefully between sycamores and oaks into a ravine, the fabric of my sundress whispering against my legs. A man was lying on his back there with a woman straddling him; she rocked and occasionally moaned with pleasure.

A rush of heat enveloped my cheeks. I headed back through the trees, cringing as twigs snapped underfoot. From the ravine, a voice called out. "Hey!" Footsteps approached.

"I'm so sorry," I said. "I didn't realize—"

My words dissolved into surprise as the man stepped into the moonlight. I knew him. A distant version of me couldn't place him, but I recognized him now.

"Well, hey there, stranger," Sheriff Proctor said. He buckled his pants as he approached. My heart thumped hard in my chest, like a fist knocking on a door.

"I didn't see anything," I said, the waver in my voice masked by a nervous laugh. "Your secret is safe with me," I promised.

That's when I saw the girl. She stood naked ten or fifteen yards behind the sheriff. As she took a few steps closer, her features came abruptly into sharp focus. So young, so bold. The sight of her hurt with such intensity that sleep was ripped away in an instant.

I sat up in bed with tears clouding my vision, my heart in a vice. *No, God. Please.*

I needed desperately for it to be a mistake, my overactive imagination. I needed to be wrong more than I'd ever needed anything in my entire miserable life. But I wasn't. I'd seen what I'd seen, and my dreams never lied. As much as I wanted to, I simply couldn't deny the truth any longer.

Mindy stirred nearby and adjusted her pillow. Her breathing deepened again while I mourned in the cover of darkness, my soul in bloody shreds.

It must've been an hour later when I finally calmed enough to sleep. I hadn't come to peace with anything, to be clear; I was just too weary to think anymore. Yet just as my eyelids tried to slide closed, movement caught my attention.

From one corner of the room, Carl Whitehorse emerged in the cloak of darkness and shuffled to the end of the bed. Eerily pale, he gave me a somber nod of greeting. His milky gaze shifted to Mindy and lingered on her sleeping form. His face contorted into a mask of sheer anguish. He knew, I realized.

Sluffing off the sheets, I got out of bed on shaky legs. Carl was angry—angry enough to exact revenge, I was certain.

But he didn't. Instead, he glared openly at me. And though he didn't speak a word, Carl's message was loud and clear. Seconds later, the bedroom door creaked open and the old man slipped into the night.

"What're you doing?" Mindy muttered.

I turned to look at her in the dim light. "Nothing, babe."

"Come back to bed then."

I didn't even bother trying to sleep after that. I stared at the ceiling, doing my best to think about nothing until the sky finally lightened.

January 7, 2019 … 1:04 p.m.

I held the phone against my ear and waited for him to do the same. "Thanks for agreeing to see me."

Jim Thompson nodded warily. His eyes were baggy, his cheeks gaunter than I remembered.

"You get much sleep in here?"

He gave me a dry scowl. "Came all this way just to see how I'm sleepin'?"

"More of a commentary on your appearance."

The old man snickered with a tinge of annoyance.

"You said something a little while back," I said. "It's been stewing in my mind ever since."

The old man smiled faintly, his irritation gone with surprising abruptness. "To be expected," he mused. "I am a font of wisdom."

Under different circumstances—and coming from anyone else—this might've drawn a laugh; I confronted the quip with deadpan eyes. "You said you were trying to protect Mindy. Not just Mindy, but me, too. You remember saying that?"

Jim leaned back in his chair, stretching the pigtailed phone cable taut.

"Thing is, I have these dreams," I explained. "I see things."

If I expected the man to be surprised, I should've known better. "I've always known you were different, Shane. Folks don't call you *Ghost Boy* for nuthin."

"Is that why you've hated me all these years? Because I'm different?"

He rewarded this with a wan smile and no reply.

"Those women, they suffered like you wouldn't believe."

The smile faded; his brow furrowed.

"Awinita," I said, scrutinizing his features for a spark of recognition. There wasn't one.

"That supposed to mean sumthin to me?"

"That was her name. The old woman you guys dragged into the woods back in '68. Alan Proctor raped her while Ralph Crowley held her down. Ray Middleton was there, too."

The disgraced sheriff swallowed and leaned far enough back

that the front legs of his chair lifted off the floor. "I don't know what you're talkin' about."

"C'mon, Jim. There's no need for secrecy anymore. It's not like things could get much worse for you."

Jim chewed his lip contemplatively. "If you really did dream about it, you must know I didn't pull the trigger."

I nodded.

"So why bring it up at all?"

"Because it proves something—something I didn't want to acknowledge. You're not a murderer. You were telling the truth about that. You didn't kill those women."

His eyebrows rose, his mouth fell slightly agape.

"It was Mindy, wasn't it?" My voice hitched, but I held strong to my resolve.

"You can't prove that," he whispered.

Again, I nodded. "Nor do I want to. This is just between us."

His eyes flicked to the door where a guard was swiping up and down the screen of his phone. Jim swallowed hard. "Sumthin wasn't right with that girl from the day she was born," he said. "She was just so damn rebellious."

"She was abused, you know."

The old man stiffened. "You dreamed that, too? 'Cause I never laid a hand on her in anger."

"Didn't say by you. And that's not the kind of abuse I'm talking about."

With troubled eyes, Jim Thompson leaned forward a bit, giving the telephone cord some slack. "You mean, like... *sexual* abuse?"

"Yeah."

He fell silent for a long moment, then looked away. "My daddy?"

"As in Alan Proctor? I thought he was your stepdad."

He waved this off. "He's the only daddy I ever knew."

I nodded.

The old man's eyes screwed shut. "Son of a bitch," he whispered. "If he was still alive, I'd rip his goddamn heart out."

"You two didn't get along, did you?"

With eyes still closed, Jim shook his head. "He was a filthy human bein'. Back in '68, that woman he killed—what was her name?"

"Awinita."

"She wasn't the first, you know. And she sure as hell wasn't the last."

"If you knew, why didn't you do something about it?"

His eyes opened, but they fell to his free hand and lingered there. "I was afraid."

Strange, I thought, to hear such words from this man. Until that moment, I'd often wondered if the great Jim Thompson was capable of something as human as fear. However bizarre, though, it made sense. For a much younger Jim Thompson, that is.

A whisper echoed deep in my gray matter. "He had something on you, didn't he?"

He smiled faintly. "Well, ain't you a regular Perry Mason."

"Crowley," I muttered. "The woman he killed... you helped him cover it up."

Jim's eyes hardened. "How could you possibly know about that?"

I said nothing.

He drifted into thought for a few seconds. At once, his expression widened. "Spence," he said with a sigh.

"I'm surprised you guys didn't take him out," I remarked. "He's one hell of a loose end."

"My daddy wanted to, believe me."

"But not you?"

"Like you said—I ain't no murderer. 'Sides, I liked Lloyd. Can't say he ever liked me, but I always looked up to him. He was everything my daddy wasn't."

"So Crowley kills a woman, drunk off his ass. What then?"

"My daddy and me, we hid her remains in that flooded house." He smiled bitterly. "Stupidest thing I've ever done. From that moment on, I was at his mercy. I couldn't do a damn thing to take him down without bringin' myself down with him."

"So how does Mindy fit in with all this?"

Jim hesitated, chewed his lip for a second. "Sure you wanna hear this?"

Not even remotely. "Yeah, I'm sure."

Jim took a deep breath. "Few years after you moved away, this kid rolled into town. Just passin' through, but he didn't get far. Came home for lunch one day to find Alice and Mindy buryin' him in the back yard."

My mouth fell agape. How could I have misjudged Alice with such abandon for all these years?

"I had to intervene. I mean, they didn't know what the hell they were doin'—leavin' trace evidence everywhere, getting' blood all over their clothes. And buryin' a damn corpse in our own back yard, for Christ's sake? In broad daylight!" He chuffed with exasperation. "So we moved it."

"Into the flooded house?"

A sad nod. "I thought at the time, anyone who discovered it would think it was the same killer. And since Crowley's victim died before Mindy was even born, no one would ever suspect her."

"So what changed?"

"Few weeks ago, Alice found that box of trophies at Mindy's apartment."

I nodded, finally seeing where he was going. "And you realized there'd been others?"

"Right."

"The majority of those were your dad's, you know."

Jim's eyebrows rose. "Guess there ain't no point askin' how the hell you'd know that, right?"

I blinked but didn't reply.

He laughed humorlessly. "Figured as much. Anyhow, I guess Mindy musta found that damn box when we were clearin' out Daddy's house after he died."

I could've corrected him on this, knowing Alan had gifted the box to Mindy. I could have, but I didn't.

"But I could tell she'd added to it," he was saying. The disgraced sheriff shook his head with a tired sigh. "When you confronted me that night at the jail? It dawned on me that she mighta hidden more bodies there. I had to be sure. Turns out I was right."

"And the others near your house?"

"Those were news to me. Alice never uttered a word about them."

I leaned back in my chair, suddenly exhausted. "So that's it, then. You're ready to take the fall for all those murders to protect Mindy."

A determined nod. "It's what you do as a parent. You protect your kids, no matter what." His gaze flicked away, the corners of his mouth twitching. "I couldn't protect Carrie. Ain't about to fail again."

I considered rewarding his candor with some of my own. Mindy and Alan had killed together at least once, after all, and Jim was clearly none the wiser. Looking back, I now consider my silence to be proof that I was finally maturing.

From nowhere, a thought struck me. "Did you kill Ray Middleton?"

Thompson wiped his cheek and straightened in his chair. "What? Now, why in the hell would you think that?"

"I spoke with a woman at the Crossroads Nursing Home just a few hours after he died. She said you paid him a visit that same morning."

Jim shrugged. "Ray was my friend. I never would've hurt him, much less killed him."

He looked like he had more to say, but he bit the rest off. I waited him out.

"He wanted to come clean," Jim relented. "About the Indian woman."

"And you were okay with that?"

Jim crossed his arms with an air of indignation. "Matter of fact, I was. I brought a tape recorder and everything. But he lost his train of thought a few minutes in, and... well, he just couldn't get the train back on the tracks."

We were silent for a few seconds, each lost in our own thoughts—our hopes and regrets.

Jim broke the spell. "I'm sorry, Shane," he muttered, his shoulders sagging. "I hounded you like a dog on a coon."

I blinked in surprise.

"You ain't such a bad guy. And I know you didn't have nuthin to do with the drownin'." He scratched his chin absently. "Deep down, I guess I've always known. It was just…" His head swayed from side to side. "Goddamn, you were just so easy to hate. I mean, it wasn't any secret that you had some kind of… *gift.*"

Combined with the apology, his admission of knowing about me—my connection to the dead rather than the more popular assumption of mental illness—left me breathless for several seconds. When I finally mustered the sense to speak, I managed a smile. "It's almost like I was asking for it, huh?"

He nodded with a sad sort of smile.

"I love your daughter, you know. We're getting married soon." My grip tightened on the phone. "I need to know, Jim. Do you think she'll do it again?"

The old man seemed to deflate, growing smaller, more and more feeble with each passing second. He let the front legs of his chair return to the floor and leaned closer to the glass between us. "I don't have an answer for that, Shane. But the fact that you even gotta ask tells me you ain't ready to be her protector."

"Maybe."

"Either way, I guess that's a risk you'll just have to take."

It was after three when I left the penitentiary in McAlester. Mindy would be off work by seven. She had dinner plans with Alyssa—it hadn't taken them long to patch things up after the anniversary. Frankly, I was grateful for the evening alone; Mindy and I had things to talk about—a wedding to plan, for Christ's sake—but I didn't have it in me just then. I was an absolute mess. Fury was building up like a supernova. I wanted to scream, to hurt someone. To destroy something.

My phone vibrated from its perch on the air vent and I answered in a daze.

It was David. "Hey, bud. Any chance you can meet for a drink? We need to talk."

I wanted to be alone, not shooting the shit like everything was fine. "I don't know, man. It's been a long day and I'm feeling pretty worn out."

The line fell silent.

"Rain check?" I offered.

"Sure," he agreed. "How about lunch tomorrow?"

I hesitated. "Yeah, okay. Sounds good." It didn't, but it bought me some time to get a grip on things.

It was half past five when I finally pulled up to my apartment. I lived three doors down from Mindy and Alyssa, my lease secured by a bloated savings account as opposed to a steady job. Mindy was supposed to move in soon—hell, she rarely slept at her place anymore. Her moving in had seemed like a no-brainer only a week ago. Now?

Funny how a little dream can change everything.

My stomach was in knots, too upset to deal with food. Out of pure muscle memory, I popped the top off a beer and took a swig, realizing too late that I didn't want that either.

I left it on the counter and crawled into bed, begging the god of shitty luck for dreamless sleep. For once, my prayers were answered.

CHAPTER 31

January 8, 2019 … 12:16 p.m.

Thanks for meeting me, Shane."

I clapped David lightly on the shoulder. "No problem, bud." A good night's sleep had done wonders for my aching heart. I wasn't sure where the peace came from, but I was grateful for it. I was also starving.

We perused our menus and sipped ice water. When the owner padded to our table, I felt my frame stiffen. This was the part where he'd ask me to leave, give me the whole *sorry, we're closed* bit. Only, he did nothing of the sort. He took our orders and headed for the kitchen without batting an eye. When he was gone, David cleared his throat.

"Listen, we're about to have a pretty big conversation, Shane. I need to know right now—can you keep your cool, or should we talk back at the station?"

I clasped my hands on the table. As far as intros went, David's seemed designed to intentionally put me on guard. His demeanor felt all wrong, too—on edge, wary. "What's up, man?"

He took a deep breath. "You might've heard the medical examiner finished the autopsies a while back."

I hadn't, but what the hell? I played along, nodding dumbly. "Um, sure. Okay."

"Thing is, there were some foreign hairs found on one of the bodies. Some skin, as well. Under her fingernails."

My stomach crawled into my throat. "Really?" I squeaked. "You'd think the water would've washed that stuff away."

He shrugged. "Sometimes we get lucky. She wasn't in there long, and she was wrapped in plastic, which slowed down decomposition."

I sipped my water and chewed on an ice cube, tried to play it cool. *She wasn't in there long.*

"Has she been identified?"

"Runaway from Joplin. Reported missing not long before you came home." He sighed through his nose, squeezing his eyes shut for a second. "Only seventeen years old."

"Jesus," I hissed.

David licked his lips. "Anyway, we sent the samples off for analysis. It took several months—it's a pretty slow process, contrary to what Hollywood would have you believe. Anyway, we finally got the results back." He swallowed nervously. "We got a match."

I held my breath.

My buddy leaned forward and splayed his fingers on the table between us. "This isn't going to be easy to hear, Shane. I wanted you to hear it from me, because it's coming out no matter what."

"What're you trying to tell me, Dave?" I asked this as if I didn't already know the answer, as if there was even a tiny chance that I could be wrong.

"The DNA recovered from the body? It's a match to Mindy Thompson."

I felt my muscles quiver with dismay.

"Are you hearing me, Shane? Do you understand what I'm telling you? All the evidence suggests that Mindy was involved in the murder of that woman. Could be others, too."

I didn't trust myself to speak, so I buried my face in my hands and said nothing at all.

David shook his head. "I'm so sorry, man. Truly."

I slumped back in my seat, deflated. "When are you planning to arrest her?"

He opened his mouth but hesitated. "The DA filed charges this morning. Mindy's already in custody by now, Shane."

A wounded glare hijacked my features. "Wait, you... you *lured* me here?"

David took a deep breath, then nodded. "I couldn't risk things blowing up with you present for the arrest. I was trying to protect you. And her."

"You son of a bitch!" Tears ping-ponged down the stubble on my cheeks. Deep down, I'd known this day would come. But I never imagined it would come so soon. The injustice of it all ravaged me inside.

David flinched at my outburst, but he stopped short of an apology. Instead, he set his jaw. "I need to ask you something, and I need a straight answer, Shane. It's important."

I wiped my eyes and tried to keep it together.

"I need to understand how you knew where those bodies were hidden."

I laughed humorlessly. "Yeah, you and me both."

David chewed his lower lip, dropped his voice. "I'm doing my best to keep you out of this, Shane. But I need your help to do that. How'd you know?"

"C'mon, Dave. You've heard all the rumors about me."

"Cut the shit, man. I wanna help you—truly I do—but you've got to set the record straight, here. Were you involved somehow?"

I considered a manufactured response but decided not to bother. What was the point? Not only was the truth too implausible to believe, I was a terrible liar. With fresh tears stinging my eyes, I slid from the booth and got to my feet.

David rose and grabbed me by the arm as I headed for the door. "I can't let you leave just yet, Shane."

"Then do what you gotta do. Arrest me. Charge me with something." A sob broke loose and I clamped my mouth shut. "Better yet, shoot me in the goddamn head, Dave. Put me out of my misery."

David's grip loosened and I wrenched free.

In the privacy of my car, a memory pounced on me. A twelve- or thirteen-year-old Mindy straddling her grandpa, moaning with pleasure. The image plunged in and out of focus with unnerving brutality, not unlike a long, dull blade to the chest. Alone in my car, I tried to catch a breath as grief overwhelmed me.

I think that was the moment when I made up my mind. There

were other contributing incidents along the way, of course—I suppose I'd been toying with the idea for most of my life—but that particular moment sealed the deal.

A life without Mindy Thompson simply wasn't a life worth living.

EPILOGUE

January 27, 2019 ... 9:44 a.m.

The Yonker's fishing enclosure is long gone, but the dock and slips remain. It sways gently in the cold breeze. I lay on my back, gazing skyward. I'm out of tears, sapped of emotion altogether. I've spent a lifetime trying to squeeze some happiness from this world, mostly to no avail. The lingering hatred, the indifference of the community—I can live with that. I've already proven that much. Yet despite all the shit this life has thrown at me, I've never been as alone as I am now.

I'm empty. A shell of a man who can no longer support the immensity of his own gravity. And I'm done trying.

I sit up to gaze across the water. Images of bodies flutter through my mind, rocking gently in the waves. A gust of cold air sweeps across the lake, raking my flesh in passing. Temperatures have been hovering in the low twenties for the last several days, the wind chill in single digits. I don't mind. The bitter cold feels right.

That's when I see her. She's chest-deep in the cove, beckoning me with open arms; my chapped lips split into a smile. Drowsiness descends on me as I struggle to my feet.

The water, she sings in my ear. *Come to the water. Come to me, my love.*

Another gust of wind ravages my flesh. I'm shivering, I realize. No matter. The water will be warm.

Hurry, child. Come to me.

I take a step toward the edge of the dock and close my eyes. The old wood creaks under my weight. No trotlines will stop me today, I tell myself.

This time, I'll get it right.

From the shore, a sobbing bellow interrupts my thoughts. "No-no-no! Don't you dare, Shane! Please, I-I'm begging you!

It's Winnie. A quick glance to shore reveals that she isn't alone; Mike and David are there, too.

"It's better this way," I call over my shoulder, inching closer to the lapping water.

Mike hops onto the gangway and strides toward me with David on his tail.

"Stop!" I bark.

"Sorry, brother," he replies without slowing. "No can do."

A moment later, Winnie is on her way, too.

Dammit.

"Please, guys. It's what I want—it's what *she* wants." Only, when I turn back to the water, the woman is gone.

Fresh tears come now, and there's no stopping them. They pound my insides to mush, ripping the strength from my limbs. Mike catches me in a tight embrace that all but crushes me. David and Winnie pile on.

"Please," I whisper through a sob. "I'm done."

Winnie presses her forehead against mine, her jowls shaking with emotion. "No, Shane. You ain't done yet. Today is the day you start livin', y'hear me? God knows you've been dyin' long enough."

I didn't want to believe Winnie, but it turns out she was right. I'm not quite done. Every day gets a little easier. I get out of bed and go through the motions. Some days, I find something to smile about. Other days, it's the motions themselves that keep me going. Their banality grounds me, even if I carry them out with complete disinterest. Over time, the good has begun to pile up on the bad.

Blessedly, the town seems to have given up its hostility toward me. When I catch someone looking my way these days, I'm more likely to receive a polite wave than a glare. I'm not sure who I have to thank for that. Maybe it isn't any one person, or maybe it isn't a person at all. Maybe it was always just a matter of time. Whatever the case, free of the burden for the first time since I was a kid, I'm seeing things differently.

The beauty of this town all but overwhelms me. It's like I'm seeing it for the first time, every day. The trees, the winding roads. The deer and songbirds. I can hardly wait for spring, when the landscape will come alive.

David and I hit the gym on weekday mornings. I can still give him a run for his money in the ring, but the rage that fueled me for so long is gone.

Mike pulled a few strings to get me hired on as a handyman for a quaint resort on Drowning Creek. Belle View. It's small and pays shit, but I don't mind. My boss is a little rough around the edges, yet kind-hearted. Funny as hell, too. I don't suppose I've had two days alike there.

The resort has an enclosed fishing dock that reminds me of Yonker's. I've never actually fished from it, but I discovered that I can see quite a ways down Drowning Creek from there. If I squint hard enough, I can even make out the spot where thirty-six kids lost their lives, along with the cove where I nearly lost mine. These days, though, I don't feel the need to look. I try to keep my gaze trained on the future now, not the past.

Winnie's a gentler soul than she used to be. She finally got around to moving into the house, by the way. She sold her RV on craigslist for pennies on the dollar, but she didn't complain much. She used some of the money for a weekend in Eureka Springs. Her relationship with Melinda turned into more of a camaraderie than a love connection, but Winnie adores their friendship.

Monday through Friday, I eat dinner with my aunt. Rain or shine, I spend Saturday mornings fishing with Mike. Saturday nights are dogeared for poker with David, Mike and Jean. I'm usually lucky to leave with my shirt. On Sundays, I drink copious amounts of coffee and read to my heart's content.

Cassie from the convenience store? She asked me on a date. I haven't decided what to do yet. Winnie thinks I should give it a shot. Mike just says, "Whatever makes you happy, bro." Like that helps.

I'm so grateful to have friends, for Winnie. Thanks to them, life isn't all bad. On the contrary, it can be quite good—even if it'll never be what I hoped for.

March 9, 2019 ... 9:55 a.m.

Today's turning into one of those unseasonably warm Saturdays, the kind that makes you long for summer. Mike and I have been fishing hard since six with no luck. I'm not bothered in the least, but we decide to call it quits anyway.

"I promised Tabitha I'd watch the kids for a bit," Mike explains. "Why don't you come on over? I make a mean grilled cheese sandwich."

It's tempting, but something calls me home. I take a rain check.

A letter from Mindy is waiting in my mailbox. I have a shoebox full of them, some read in haste, others indulged over and over until the folds have come apart. I tried to visit her a few times, in the beginning. She wouldn't see me. I don't expect that to change, but I haven't given up hope. In the meantime, I settle for these little scraps of paper. What else can I do?

I love Mindy Thompson. I have almost since I can remember, and I'll probably love her until the day I die. But you can love someone with every ounce of your being and still never understand them.

I see that now, as well as how unhealthy committing to that kind of love is.

So, I'm doing my best to become someone new. Someone defined by other virtues. A man who finds happiness in the little things, who looks for the good in people. A man who values the good in himself, even if others don't.

A man who loves Mindy Thompson but can survive without her.

I kick back with a Dr. Pepper and settle in to read Mindy's letter. I'm a page in when I notice the little boy in my kitchen. He beckons me to follow and darts to the front door. The back of his head isn't shaped right, I can't help but notice. His curly brown hair is matted against a crater in his skull, glistening in bloody clumps.

I don't want to follow him, and if I ignore him long enough, I'm pretty sure he'll leave. But as he waits patiently by the door, eyes pleading, it finally dawns on me. Why the Lady of the Water spared me—not once, but twice.

For my entire adult life, I've moped along with no real direction, trying to suffocate what differentiates me from everyone else. But now, I have to wonder… what if my gift—however macabre—is more than just a tacky parlor trick? What if using it for good has been my destiny all along?

Before I can change my mind, I push back from the table and get to my feet. "Okay, little man. You've got my attention."

NOW WHAT?

Thanks so much for reading Last Breath! If you liked this book, would you please consider posting an honest review to your point of sale? Reviews are a great way for readers to discover new books, and the author would greatly appreciate it.

ABOUT THE AUTHOR

Lincoln Chase is a fiction writer and stay-at-home dad. He loves books, movies, coffee and the occasional cat-video binge on You-Tube. In his spare time, he—wait... what the hell is spare time? Okay, if Lincoln had spare time, he would undoubtedly enjoy baking cookies, long walks on a beach and driving a car with more than one hubcap.

ALSO BY LINCOLN CHASE

Deadline
Tide Pool
Afflicted

THE DOMINIC WOLFE TALES:
Kinda Sorta Dead, Book 1
Half Past Crazy, Book 2
Wrong Side of Chaos, Book 3
Better Late Than Stupid, Book 4
Split Shift, A Dominic Wolfe Short
Casting Shadows, A Dominic Wolfe Short

Bringing new adventures to life, one word at a time.

www.designvaultpress.com

www.ingramcontent.com/pod-product-compliance
Lightning Source LLC
Chambersburg PA
CBHW021328250626

47155CB00002B/633